SALOME

Servant Siblings Series: Book 7

JENIFER JENNINGS

Editor: Jill Monday

Scripture quotations and paraphrases are taken from The Holy Bible, English Standard Version, Copyright © 2001 by Crossway, a publishing ministry of Good News Publishers.

This book is a work of historical fiction based closely on real people and events recorded in the Holy Bible. Details that cannot be historically verified are purely products of the author's imagination. Any resemblance to actual persons, living or dead, or actual events is purely coincidental.

ISBN: 978-1-954105-36-2

For Jill,
I pray God continues to use you in mighty ways.

"But Saul was ravaging the church, and entering house after house, he dragged off men and women and committed them to prison."

-Acts 8:3

CHAPTER 1

35 A.D., Jerusalem

Salome dug at her arm where the worn sackcloth irritated her skin. The mourning material was certainly doing its job of reminding her to be grateful for joyful days. Today wasn't one of them.

She slowed her pace, the basket against her hip heavy with provisions. Its frayed woven handle bit into her palm, the coarse fibers pricking her skin as she held it tight. Every jostle sent an enticing fragrance of her mother's fresh-baked loaves drifting up from under the cloths keeping them warm. Nestled next to the stack was a large wedge of hard goat cheese and a selection of dried fruits and fish. These were intended to fill the stomach of a recent widow. Little comfort for the woman who had lost her beloved life-partner and financial security but comfort nonetheless.

Salome recalled how her mother's lashes shimmered with unshed tears when she handed Salome the basket. Mary knew the pain of losing a spouse, and Salome remembered her father's absence with each passing harvest. Her father never got the chance to celebrate one with her, as he'd done for all her older siblings. Salome spent a lifetime grieving for a man she never knew.

She shifted the basket to her other hip and ducked into the olive grove. The garden surrounding the grove was meticulously tended and teamed with life. Ancient olive trees provided shade for a vast collection of plants and homes for birds and other creatures. Musky and sweet earthy scents mingled in this private space.

The sturdy trees would make excellent climbing challenges for Salome. These were Goliaths gracing the Jerusalem hillside compared to the puny ones that dotted the Galilean landscape near her home in Nazareth. Alas, this was not the time to gird her loins and scurry up the branches. Perhaps if she endeared herself to the owners, they might approve of a future attempt.

Deep inside the garden, she came upon the tomb. She quickened her steps, urged forward to take another peek inside as she'd done on countless days. Stooping at the gaping mouth of the cave, she gazed into the darkness. When her eyes adjusted to the dim, she beheld the empty place where her oldest brother had lain. The stone table was bare. The tomb was still empty.

A smile lifted the corners of her mouth. She envisioned the two divine messengers sitting at either end of the table, just as Mary Magdalene had described. What must it have been like to see the lightning-bright beings that glorious morning?

The weight of the basket on her hip reminded her she could not linger. There was much to be done.

She sighed, allowing herself a few more heartbeats of gazing before she straightened. Lifting her free hand, she rubbed the broken seal on the large stone. Two years of weather had worn away Pilate's official symbol. All that remained was the waxy smear of red that once threatened death to anyone who dared break it.

Renewed, Salome made her way to the stone house in the grove's heart. Stopping at the open door, she hesitated. It was customary to call out a blessing before being invited inside a home, but with the family sitting *shiva* for their lost patriarch, the courtesy seemed inappropriate. The week-long mourning practice allowed the open door to stand as its own invitation for those who wished to visit the family. She wiped the smile from her lips and stepped inside.

Warm lamp light bathed her face as she searched for the members of the house. The scent of burning oil was heavy and sweet as she pushed deeper inside. There, in the largest room, two figures sat together clothed in sackcloth and shrouded in sorrow. Salome's chest tightened.

The older woman perched upon a bright blue pillow, reminding Salome so much of her mother. Similar build, similar facial structures, bright eyes, but this woman had certainly seen fewer harvests.

Next to her was a young man who looked about the same age as Salome. His broad shoulders seemed out of place for the rest of him, and his chin was only just producing patches of hair. His eyes, though similar in shape and color to his mother's, did not hold the same brightness.

Their hushed conversation halted at her approach. "*Shalom.*" Salome lifted a silent prayer with the greeting. If only she could infuse this family with peace as easily as speaking the word. "I'm Salome bat Joseph. Simon Peter sent me." She lifted the basket, hoping the gesture would put them at ease.

"Of course." The woman motioned to a low table across the room. "Please call me Miriam. It seems more fitting now than Mary."

They even share the same name, Lord. Salome's thoughts returned to her mother. *You should have sent her. I know nothing of the path a widow walks.*

Baskets of all shapes and sizes sprawled across the

surface of the low table, indicating the family's status in Jerusalem. Everyone who knew anything got their oil from the family who owned the grove near the Mount of Olives. It seemed many in the community had come to give their support to the family, though there didn't seem to be anyone sitting with them today.

Odd. Salome tucked her basket among the others and elected to sit on a tan pillow near Miriam.

Two sets of eyes settled on her. She never knew what to say at times like this. It was easier to simply sit and let others provide comforting words to the grieving. Every day, more needy people strained the resources of the followers of the Way. This was Salome's first time visiting a widow alone. Peter and James assured her she was ready, but staring into the watery eyes of two people who had just placed their husband and father on a stone slab set hornets loose in her stomach.

"Simon Peter sends his greetings." Salome shifted on the plump pillow. "He promised to visit when he gets an opportunity."

"He's very busy." Miriam hummed to herself. "People are busier than ever."

Salome moved her gaze to the young man.

"Oh, I don't know where my manners are today." Miriam placed a gentle hand on her son's arm. "This is my son, John ben Micah."

John lowered his chin. "Most people call me John Mark."

She nodded a return bow as an uneasy silence settled on her shoulders. She was supposed to bring this hurting family comfort and here she was with an empty mouth. "Simon Peter tells me you're related to Barnabas."

"Who?" Miriam stared at her.

"Sorry." Salome shook her head. "Joseph, the disciples call him Barnabas."

Miriam hummed again. "Barnabas suits him better. I like it." A slight smile brought more light to her eyes. "His mother is my sister. Our family resides mostly in Cyprus. Though I've lived in Jerusalem since I married…"

Salome saw some of the brightness leave Miriam's eyes. She chided herself for bringing up family.

Miriam turned to John Mark. "I'm going to get our guest something to eat." She rose.

"Oh, please don't trouble yourself." Salome raised an open palm to her. "The provisions I brought are for your family. I've already broken my fast."

"We have plenty." Miriam waved toward the piles on the table. "Better to share than see it go to waste."

Salome couldn't argue. The family seemed well taken care of. Why had James sent her here?

She returned her attention to John Mark. He twisted the ragged end of his sackcloth tunic. She opened her mouth to say something but snapped it closed, fearing she'd choose the wrong topic again.

"I was there that night."

John Mark's unprompted statement sent a chill up Salome's back. "Pardon?"

"The night they arrested your brother." He slowly looked up at her. "I was there."

Salome's throat constricted.

"I tried to stop them, the soldiers." He dropped his gaze and continued to twist the dark material through his fingers. "I heard the commotion and saw them trying to take Jesus away. I knew He had done nothing wrong. He couldn't have. I tried to stop them." A single, large tear rolled down his cheek.

"You couldn't have stopped a band of Roman soldiers and Temple guards. Even Peter tried and…well…it didn't work out."

"They all ran." John Mark pounded his fist into his open palm. "All His followers just ran away. How could they do that to Him?" His dark eyes lifted, demanding an answer.

Salome had none. How could she answer things even she did not understand?

Miriam handed Salome a chunk of torn bread and part of the hard cheese. "They're simple men, son."

Salome accepted the food from her but held onto the pieces instead of eating them.

Miriam offered another portion to John Mark.

He shook his head.

"Eat." Miriam shoved them into his hands. "It'll do you well." She sank back into her pillow. "We mustn't be angry about the choices of others. All of us, at some point in our lives, flee when we should stand. After all, the men came back, and they've continued to do mighty deeds since then."

"I suppose." John Mark whispered a simple blessing and bit into the bread.

Salome nibbled on the cheese while the hornets in her stomach protested. In a matter of moments, she reminded a widow of her greatest loss and set fire to a young man's anger. Some comforter she was turning out to be.

CHAPTER 2

After forcing down the bread and cheese, Salome brushed crumbs from her lap. The food helped quiet her raging stomach hornets, but she still had no words for the grieving family. What sentiment could possibly ease their wounded hearts? What truth would provide the balm they needed during this season of loss?

"Simon Peter tells me you lost your father."

Salome gazed up into Miriam's red-rimmed eyes. "When I was very young."

"How young?" John Mark's voice cracked.

"Before I could even form a memory of him." Salome recalled her family's stories. "He died in a quarry accident when I was just an infant. I only know my father through what my *ima* and siblings have shared with me."

John Mark's cheeks flamed. "My abba was a great man. A faithful man."

"Then I'm sure he reclines with Abraham." Salome smiled but quickly forced her lips down. This was not the time to be smiling.

"How can you be sure?" John Mark wiped his face. "How can anyone be sure?"

Salome opened her mouth, then pushed her lips into a thin line. Would anything she say offer a measure of comfort? A thought pressed its way forward. "May I tell you one of my brother's stories?"

John Mark nodded and set his chin in his hands.

"Jesus told of a rich man who was clothed in purple and fine linens and who feasted every day. At his gate lay a poor man named Lazarus."

John Mark lifted his head. "From Bethany?"

"No." Salome held up her hand. "Another man named Lazarus. A poor man covered with sores who craved the crumbs that fell from the rich man's table. The poor man even had dogs lick his sores." Her nose flinched. "Both men died, but the poor man was carried by Adonai's messengers to Abraham's side while the rich man was taken to be tormented."

She stole a glance at Miriam, who seemed as drawn into the story as John Mark. "While the rich man was being tormented, he saw Abraham far off and Lazarus at his side. He called out, 'Father Abraham, have mercy on me, and send Lazarus to dip the end of his finger in water and cool my tongue, for I am in anguish in this flame.'"

John Mark huffed. "Sounds like the rich man was still considering Lazarus as low as a servant even after death made them equals."

"True, but Abraham said, 'Child, remember that you in your lifetime received good things, and Lazarus bad things; but now he is comforted here, and you are in anguish. A great chasm is also fixed between us that no one can cross.'"

John Mark tapped a rhythm on his knee. "So, Abraham told the rich man there was a chasm in Sheol that could not be crossed?"

"Yes, and then the rich man said, 'I beg you, Father Abraham, send him to my father's house—for I have five brothers—so that he may warn them, lest they also come to this place of torment.'"

"At least the rich man seemed concerned for his siblings, even though it still sounds like he's trying to get Abraham to order Lazarus around like a servant."

Salome nodded. She had similar thoughts when she first heard the story. "But Abraham said, 'They have Moses and the prophets; let them hear them.' And the rich man said, 'No, Father Abraham, but if someone goes to them from the dead, they will repent.' Abraham said to him, 'If they do not hear Moses and the prophets, neither will they be convinced if someone should rise from the dead.'"

She gazed between Miriam and John Mark, who both held unknowing gazes. "Don't you see? My brother's story shows us that our destiny beyond Sheol is determined by our decisions in this life. If your father was a faithful man to Adonai then, even though he's been swallowed by death, he reclines with Father Abraham."

"It's a pleasant story." John Mark lifted his shoulder. "But does that make it true?"

"Jesus believed it to be true."

"So, you think my father reclines with Father

Abraham because of his faithfulness?"

"I think your father reclines with Father Abraham because of Adonai's faithfulness. If Moses and the prophets have taught us anything, it's that Adonai provides the way to Himself. We don't forge it, but we have the choice to follow it."

"Is that why Jesus' followers call themselves Way Followers?"

"Jesus said He is The Way, and we are called to follow Him. Way Followers."

Miriam rose from her pillow and moved toward the low table. She placed her palms on the surface and leaned over the abundance. "There are others who could benefit from this bounty."

Salome held her tongue. She wondered whether it was a question or a statement, or whether the story had offended the woman she was sent to comfort.

Miriam hung her head. "We've been blessed beyond measure." She slowly turned to face Salome. "Could you send a message to the other widows or anyone you know who is in need? Tell them to come to our table." Tears raced down her face. "If they can't come, I'll send a cart to bring them here. We must share what Adonai has given."

The hornets in Salome's stomach stirred again. She hadn't shared the story to guilt this widow into giving away her provisions. She merely tried to comfort a son who was unsure of his father's place. Rising, she stood beside Miriam. "We would appreciate anything you share. There are many needs, but these gifts were intended for you."

"Then they are mine to do with as I please. Though I have one condition." Miriam held up a finger.

"Condition?"

"Yes." Miriam reached for Salome's arm. "You must continue to come and share more of your brother's stories with those who feast from our table."

"Me? But I haven't even done well in providing you with comfort. I don't even know all my brother's stories." The internal hornets migrated to her chest. "I can't speak to a crowd."

"Shalom." Miriam gripped her arm. "Adonai has given you the perfect words to comfort us." She looked at her son. "See."

Salome turned to John Mark. There was a spark of brightness in his dry eyes that matched his mother's.

"I think it's a great way to honor Abba." John Mark's lips quivered into a slight grin. "He'd be proud of us."

The buzzing in Salome's chest quieted. "The story was comforting?"

"Yes." Miriam gave her arm another squeeze before releasing it. "And convicting. You reminded John of Adonai's faithfulness, and you reminded me that we should share blessings. It's not like I can take any of this with me to Sheol." She waved over the baskets. "But I can use it to fill empty bellies while you spread the balm of Jesus' stories to wounded souls as you've done for us."

"I don't know." Salome rubbed her itchy arm. "My brothers and Jesus' followers are much better at sharing His stories. They sent me to bring provisions and sit with you. I don't think I'm supposed to be speaking to gatherings."

"I believe you are." Miriam's eyes shimmered. "You have a gift for stories as Jesus did."

The comparison to her Messiah brother sent warmth through her, but the raging fight in her stomach and chest doused the flame. "I'll speak with James and Peter."

"Wonderful." Miriam clapped.

Salome left the mother and son before they could negotiate any more out of her. She took the long way through the garden, passing by the empty tomb again.

Instead of stopping at the entrance, she went inside and sat on the table. Rubbing her fingertips over the cool stone, she sighed to herself. "I'm not like you, Jesus. I can't speak to crowds. No one will listen to me. No one ever listens to me."

The last words Jesus spoke before the clouds snatched Him away flooded her soul. *But you will receive power when the Holy Spirit has come upon you, and you will be my witnesses in Jerusalem and in all Judea and Samaria, and to the end of the earth.*

She closed her eyes and recalled her brother's face. "Does that promise include me, brother?"

CHAPTER 3

The following morning, in Priest Theodotos' borrowed kitchen, Salome attempted to shove another loaf of bread into her already overflowing basket.

"Save some for the rest of us."

She turned to see Hiram leaning against the doorframe. "Why? Do you still have growing to do?"

"I've been gone all this time, and that's how you greet me?"

Heat rose up Salome's neck, causing her to return her attention to her task.

Two years ago, Hiram disappeared around the same time as her brother Simon. No one would tell her what they knew about why either left, but she heard whispered conversations about Hiram's absence. He'd come searching for her the day he left. He returned two weeks ago with conversations reserved for her brothers. This was the first time since his sudden reappearance that he addressed her.

Without warning, he was next to her. Too close. She looked up into his dark eyes that seemed to hold back a flood of thoughts. She wasn't sure if she wanted to be the one to release them.

Hiram reached around her and pulled the protruding loaf from the bag. He tore off a chunk with his teeth and slowly chewed. "James tells me you're helping the widow who owns the olive grove on the mount."

She adjusted some items in the basket to avoid his critical gaze. "That's my assigned task."

"He also mentioned you asked permission to do some teaching." He took another large bite of the bread.

Her stomach flopped. Why had James told Hiram of Miriam's plea for her to share her brother's stories?

"I don't think you should do it."

His bold declaration startled her. "Pardon?"

"I don't think you should do it." He tore another chunk off the loaf and chewed without further explanation.

"I have James' permission...and Peter's." She looked over her shoulder as if to call the two men as witnesses to her claim.

"That doesn't mean you should do it."

She squinted at him. "Why not?"

"Saul."

The name sent a shiver down her back. Saul was the reason her brother Simon had fled to Damascus only days ago. The Pharisee's name was becoming a frightful word among Way Followers. Some dared not speak it, choosing rather harsh replacements instead. "He doesn't scare me."

"He should." Hiram tossed the last piece of bread into his mouth. "The council has given him permission to arrest men *and women*." His emphasis on the last two words caused crumbs to drop from his mouth into his thick beard.

Salome would have chuckled at the sight if her thoughts were not being invaded by the serpent grin of Saul.

Though her conversation with James and Peter about Miriam's request had been brief and encouraging, Salome went to sleep unsure of her answer. Staring into the firm face of Hiram and his fear-filled opinions solidified her resolve.

She lifted the basket from the table and pushed past him. "I have to do this."

Hiram halted her with a firm grip on her arm.

She glanced at his hand and traced his muscular arm up to his face. "Let me go."

"Why do you feel the need to do this?"

"It's what my brother would have wanted." She twisted out of his grasp. "Wants."

"Your brother would have wanted you cared for. Settled. Worrying about not burning a meal for your husband while mediating spats between children, not if you're going to be arrested for telling His stories."

A vision of family swept across her mind. She'd been too young and poor to dream of such things so soon. "What are you saying?"

For the first time since entering the kitchen, Hiram broke his gaze. "Nothing."

"Nothing?"

He released her arm and raised a sheepish glance. "James told me this Miriam lady has a kid your age."

"And?"

"Are you interested in him? You know. In that way?"

"We're simply friends." She considered the young man. "He lost his father. I know what that's like." She fixed a challenging stare on him. "What does it matter to you?"

"It doesn't." He folded his arms across his chest.

His denial didn't fool her. The red racing up the sides of his neck spoke much louder than his words. He looked more like a boy standing before her than even the younger John Mark. The only clues she had of the location of Hiram's disappearance were his much tanner skin and the intense gaze of a man who'd seen more than he cared to see.

"What if someone were to offer to get you out of all this?" Hiram rubbed the back of his neck. "Take you far away from Jerusalem. Maybe start a new life somewhere else?"

"Like Nicolaus has done with Lydia? Taken her to Antioch to hide from Saul?"

"Exactly."

"But Nicolaus married Lydia first."

"Yes, well…" The red reached all the way to his ears.

"I appreciate your concern, Hiram." She set her sandals toward the doorway. "But my big brother has taken care of me all my life. Death couldn't loosen His grip on me, and nothing else will either."

The fresh air on the walk from the priest's villa in the city to the stone home in the olive grove did much to clear Salome's mind. Hiram's words had caused a tangle of conflicting emotions and thoughts. He spoke as if he cared deeply for her, yet treated her like a child. Most of the people in her life treated her as such. Even though James and Peter had pushed her to make visits on her own, she'd overheard their whispered concerns about her abilities.

Hiram spoke of fleeing, but she wasn't sure if he'd ever consider marrying someone else. Not after what happened to his first betrothed years ago.

Across the Kidron Valley, the olive trees waved to her with their shimmering leaves before she reached the garden. They stood like old friends, welcoming her, beckoning her to come.

Nearing the garden, a gentle breeze rustled through the leaves, carrying the distant hum of insects and the occasional chirping of birds perched in the trees. Salome could hear the quiet murmur of water from a nearby stream mingling with the conversations of workers tending the grove. This place was so alive and yet so at peace.

Salome caught the faint smell of rosemary and thyme, their earthy aroma blended with the aromatic olive buds. The rich fragrance of the sun-warmed earth completed the scent of the grove, grounding her in its peace. She drew near to a large tree and ran her fingers through the growing shoots surrounding it.

"Shalom."

She followed the call to where John Mark dropped from a branch onto the ground in front of her. "Shalom." Her gaze lifted to where he had descended. Some of the limbs held small, cream-colored buds. "Do you climb often?"

"How do you think we get the olives out of the trees? Or prune the branches?"

"I know nothing of olive harvest," she teased. "I'm a sister of craftsmen."

"During the harvest season, we lay baskets under the trees. The young ones climb up and shake the branches." He gestured his explanation, setting out unseen baskets and pretending to shake the limbs. "Whatever falls into the baskets, we harvest. Those in need gather whatever falls onto the ground."

Salome imagined the fun of climbing trees to shake the branches of their bounty. She would have gladly volunteered to help with such a task if it meant she could spend her days climbing.

"I've spent many years in these trees helping my father harvest." John Mark let his gaze return to her. "Guess I will be the one leading the next harvest instead of climbing."

Her heart ached for him. The weight of responsibility and sorrow bent his shoulders.

"So," he straightened some, "come for a walk

among my gardens?"

"You could say that." She lifted the basket from her hip. "Got more provisions for your family."

"Ima told you we have plenty."

"She's also planning to share with every hungry mouth in Jerusalem. She could use all we can spare."

John Mark chuckled.

Salome encircled the massive tree at a slow pace. "Why do you plant rosemary and thyme near the trees?"

"You have a good eye for plants." He bent to pluck a sprig of rosemary and lifted it to his nose. "Rosemary helps attract certain insects that pollinate the olive trees and repel unwanted pests, while thyme helps give back to the soil."

"That's quite wonderful."

"It can be." He rolled the sprig between his fingers, releasing the delicate scent of the oil into the air. "If you know each plant well enough, you can create an environment in which they can all thrive."

"It's kind of that way with people." She brushed her free hand through the rosemary bushes. "We all have different things we're good at and putting some of us together can produce thriving results, but put some people together and well..."

"They can poison each other."

Salome hummed her agreement.

"Have you ever seen an olive press before?"

She shook her head.

"Follow me." John Mark led her to the large press. "It's quiet most of the year, but we couldn't produce our oil without it."

The olive press loomed large in the clearing ahead, a massive stone slab with grooves carved into its surface. A circular millstone attached to a wooden beam sat motionless in the groove.

"We fasten a donkey there." John Mark pointed to the beam. "The millstone turns the olives into a paste that we collect in baskets." He continued toward another open area where another large beam stuck out from a stone construction. "We stack the baskets here." He pointed to a place under the beam. "Then we add weights there." He moved toward the end of it. "And collect the runoff into jars there." He pointed between the two spaces. "We press the paste three times."

"Three?"

"The first press produces the purest oil. Those drippings are taken to the Temple for the lamps and anointing oil. We perform the other two pressings to ensure we extract every drop of oil from the olives."

"I didn't realize you could press olives that many times."

"We use olive oil for so many things, to light our lamps, cooking, for healing benefits, and more. If we didn't crush them so many times, we would never receive the full measure of their blessings."

"I never thought of it that way."

"It's not harvest season yet. The buds are only just arriving, but would you like to taste last year's pressing?"

"I'd be honored."

John Mark led her to the storehouse. Clay jars of varying sizes filled the stone room. He chose one and brought it to her. "Let me see your finger."

Salome lifted her finger out to him.

He expertly punctured the wax seal and let a small golden drop drip onto her skin like liquid sunshine.

She raised her finger to her mouth and licked the luscious droplet. The bitterness was sharp, but soon gave way to a fruity richness, the taste of the earth itself captured in that single drop. "That's delicious."

He warmed the bottle in his hand and smeared the wax closed before returning the jar to its shelf. "Try one of these." He pulled another jar, lifted the cloth wrapping, and produced a single olive. "Ima brines some of them."

Salome accepted the olive and popped it into her mouth. The oval burst open with a perfect wave of bitterness and salt on her tongue.

"Better with Ima's goat cheese, but not bad on their own." He partook of one before returning the jar to its place.

"John?" Miriam's call entered the room.

"Better see what she needs." John Mark motioned to the doorway. "Don't want her thinking I'm in here eating all our supplies."

Salome laughed and headed out of the room.

Miriam met them at the doorway. "My dear girl, I'm so glad to see you."

She lifted her basket. "I brought you more provisions."

"Does that mean you've agreed to share your brother's stories?"

"I will try."

"Wonderful." Miriam beamed. "Why don't you accompany me to the market? I was just loading up a cart."

"Right now?" Salome's stomach buzzed with fear.

Miriam accepted the basket from her and handed it to her son. "I can sell oil while you pour out stories in front of my booth."

Salome flicked a pleading glance at John Mark.

"Better agree." He smirked. "I've seen her throw sacks into the cart. She might do the same to you if you don't."

CHAPTER 4

Salome navigated the narrow streets of Jerusalem beside Miriam's cart. Her worn sandals occasionally caught on the uneven stones that jutted out from the ancient roadway. These paths through the Lower City were the same ones her ancestors had trod and hordes of other Jews before the construction of Jerusalem. If the stones under her could speak, would they offer wisdom or cynicism for all they've seen?

The streets were dusty and filled with refuse, a far cry from the perfumed air of the Temple Mount in the distance. Drawing near, the air grew thick with the scent of incense, but underneath it, Salome could smell the sharp tang of animals and sweat. A shrill blast of the shofar sounded around her, calling the faithful to prayer. Its echo mingled with the lowing of cattle and bleating of sheep being led to the Temple for sacrifice.

Above her, the sun beat down relentlessly; the heat radiating off the stone walls of the city like an oven. Salome wiped the sweat from her brow, wishing for a cool breeze as they made their way to the market.

Rounding the last building, the trading street opened before her. Rhythmic chants of merchants and customers haggling over prices collided while vendors shouted their best offers from both sides of the street.

A pair of Roman soldiers marched down the row. Their hobnailed sandals clapped against the stones, forcing the crowd to part in uneasy silence like the waters before Moses. Their armor glinted in the sunlight, and their hands rested casually on the hilts of their swords. The message was subtle but clear—Caesar's law ruled Jerusalem, not Moses'.

Salome hid her eyes, like many others, allowing the soldiers to pass without a glance. In their absence, the flow of people returned as if Moses had lowered his staff.

Booths burst with colors—red and yellow spices piled high in clay bowls, green herbs draped over baskets, and the merchants' earth-tone tunics clashed near the polished armor of the Roman soldiers. Children ran through the crowds, their laughter mixing with the bleating of sheep. Even the variety of faces wove a beautiful tapestry over the market street.

Miriam pulled her cart to the side and set up a booth to sell her oil.

Salome assisted by carefully setting out each precious jar.

Giving an approving nod, Miriam shooed her to the front of the booth. "I'll handle the buyers; you reach the seekers."

The familiar buzzing in Salome's stomach twisted her insides. She attempted to open her mouth, but her thoughts were empty. Slamming her lips shut, she closed her eyes. *I can't do this, brother. I'm no teacher.*

"Speak, Salome," Miriam's voice broke through her darkness. "Just speak."

Slowly, Salome opened her eyes. "A sower went out to sow," her voice was low and cracked.

"Louder."

She took a deep breath and tried again, "A sower went out to sow." Daring a peek, she saw two women at a nearby booth glance in her direction. "And as he sowed, some seeds fell along the path, and the birds came and devoured them." She moved her hand in front of her as if spreading unseen seeds. "Other seeds fell on rocky ground, where they did not have much soil, and immediately they sprang up, but since they had no depth of soil when the sun rose they were scorched. And since they had no root, they withered away."

A group of children halted and turned their attention to her.

Salome moved toward them. "Other seeds fell among thorns, and the thorns grew up and choked them. Other seeds fell on good soil and produced grain, some a hundredfold, some sixty, and some thirty. He who has ears, let him hear."

One of the little boys pointed to the side of his head. "I have ears."

The boy next to him pushed his shoulder. "That's not what she means."

Other people drew closer, sending Salome's stomach hornets to swarm in her chest. She felt something pull on her tunic. Looking down, she spotted the little boy.

He wiped his runny nose on the back of his arm. "Do you need help planting seeds?"

Salome couldn't help but yield to the smile tugging at her lips. "Would you like to hear the meaning of the story?"

His dark curls bounced with his nods.

She bent toward him. "This is the meaning. When anyone hears the word of the kingdom and does not understand it, the evil one comes and snatches away what has been sown in his heart." She made a snatching motion near him. "This is what was sown along the path."

His little hands flew to his chest with a gasp.

"As for what was sown on rocky ground," she straightened, "this is the one who hears the word and immediately receives it with joy." She caught the eyes of one woman from the next booth. "Yet he has no root in himself, but endures for a while, and when tribulation or persecution arises on account of the word, immediately he falls away."

Salome allowed her focus to hold the young woman's for a few more heartbeats before moving her gaze on to others. "As for what was sown among thorns, this is the one who hears the word, but the cares of the world and the deceitfulness of riches choke the word, and it proves unfruitful." Her attention fell on a group of Pharisees moving closer but keeping their distance from the growing crowd. "As for what was sown on good soil, this is the one who hears the word and understands it. He bears fruit and yields, in one case a hundredfold, in another sixty, and in another thirty." She glanced over her shoulder at Miriam.

The older woman inclined her head toward Salome.

"Tell us another one." The little boy yanked at her tunic again. "We want another."

Salome paced in front of Miriam's booth, sharing more stories. People ebbed and flowed around her, but many stayed to hear every one of her tales. The crowd grew larger, engulfing Miriam's booth and the surrounding others.

"What is the meaning of this?"

Salome halted as the crowd parted enough to allow a Pharisee through.

The young boy looked up at the religious leader. "She's a good storyteller, and you ruined her story."

With a wave of his hand, the Pharisee dismissed the child. "Return to your parents." His nose twitched. "As for the rest of you, clear out."

"We want to hear more stories," another child argued.

Shouts of agreement spread through the group.

"We can't have this display in our market." The Pharisee lifted his long, boney fingers toward the patrolling Roman soldiers. "We don't want to attract any unnecessary attention."

"Forgive me." Salome stepped closer. "These people do not gather for show, but to hear."

The Pharisee's left eyebrow rose in an arch. "Hear what?"

Salome's cheeks warmed. "My brother's stories of the coming kingdom."

He puffed out his chest. "And just who is your brother?"

"Jesus of Nazareth."

Salome recognized the voice calling out behind the Pharisee. *Saul.* His deep, edged tone sent her body shaking.

Stepping around the Pharisee in front of her, Saul met her face to face. "She's a sister of the dead Nazarene who the Romans crucified for his seditious ideas."

While the hornets in her stomach stung, a growl started in her chest. She squinted up at Saul. "My brother is Messiah."

"Your brother is dead." His lips curled upward. "And you'll join him in his tomb if you're not careful."

The growl in her chest spread down into her stomach, warring with the swarm. "He's no longer in that tomb."

"Oh, that's right." Saul's smirk grew. "His followers stole his body. Probably so they could feast more on his flesh."

Salome's growl clawed at her throat.

Saul spun toward the crowd. "Nothing more to

hear today." He waved them away. "Return to your trading."

Salome's throat burned with a fire she couldn't contain. "The prophet Isaiah said, 'You will indeed hear but never understand, and you will indeed see but never perceive.'"

"Silence," Saul barked at her.

"'For this people's heart has grown dull.'"

"I'm warning you, woman." Saul towered over her. "Speak another word, and you will regret it."

The burning fire in her throat raged. "'With their ears they can barely hear, and their eyes they have closed.'"

Saul wagged his finger in her face. "Not another word from you."

Salome leveled her gaze at him. "'Lest they should see with their eyes and hear with their ears and understand with their heart and turn, and I would heal them.'"

"Enough." Saul motioned to a group of Temple guards. "Arrest her."

Two guards rushed Salome, grabbing her arms and pinning them to her sides. She struggled against their hold.

Miriam came out from behind her booth. "You can't do this."

"Take her away," Saul ordered the guards and continued to dismiss the crowd.

The Temple guards forced Salome's steps forward.

She wrenched against them to see Miriam.

The woman mouthed apologies as the crowd pushed her back.

Salome struggled against the two men's hold, but her strength was not enough to overcome them. Silently, she yielded to their leading.

Nearing the Temple complex, sounds of prayers, singing, and shofar blasts heralded her approach. The guards led her up the enormous staircase and toward the Chamber of Hewn Stone.

On the other side of the large, wooden doors sat several members of the Sanhedrin around the semi-circled room. Two scribes barely lifted their quills at her approach. High Priest Joseph ben Caiaphas sat at the front of the room.

Every eye turned in her direction as the guards led her toward him.

Caiaphas lifted himself as he glared around the armored men. "Saul? What is this?"

Saul pressed past Salome and her armored escorts. "The accused is Salome bat Joseph. Arrested in the market on charges of disturbing the public order and spreading treasonous claims."

Settling back into his seat, Caiaphas waved them forward. "I'm sure you have witnesses to these claims."

"Of course." Saul motioned for two men to step forward. "Hear their claims for yourself."

Salome recognized the two men as merchants from the market.

"It's true, High Priest Caiaphas." One of them stepped forward. "This woman was gathering a crowd with wild tales of a coming kingdom against Caesar."

"We all heard her," the other seller added. "Her attempts to spread false ideas were prohibiting people from peacefully making their purchases."

"You see, High Priest." Saul spread out his hands. "This woman is endeavoring to spread the false claims of her brother, a failed prophet who was crucified by Rome. It seems she's attempting to walk his path and sacrificing public peace to do so."

Salome's stomach tightened. Where was the boldness she felt in the market? The stinging internal hornets felt like they were injecting poison into her veins, stealing her voice and her strength. Where was the fire that brought forth the words of Isaiah?

One member of the council rose from the stone steps and came toward her.

Salome looked up into the eyes of Nicodemus. A man who'd spent several evenings bringing question after question to her brother but never seemed truly satisfied with the answers Jesus provided him.

Nicodemus moved to whisper in her ear. "I didn't stand up for your brother when I should have." He sighed. "The least I can do is stand here for you now."

Her lips quivered in the absence of words.

"Do you have something to add, Nicodemus?" Caiaphas' tone held a challenging edge.

Pulling back only enough to meet her gaze,

Nicodemus continued to whisper, "I will speak for you, but you must choose what you value more, your freedom or your convictions. Don't let what happened to your brother happen to you, too."

Her jaw ached, but her mouth was empty. She hung her head.

"A wise choice." Nicodemus turned to address Caiaphas. "High Priest, where are those who would speak to this young woman's innocence?" He gestured largely toward her. "Does not our law require the testimony of her innocence to be heard before her guilt?"

Caiaphas glanced at Saul. "Well? Do you have witnesses to her innocence?"

"We are here."

Salome turned to see several men from the crowd marching toward her.

"High Priest Caiaphas," the leader bowed, "we're here to speak on behalf of this woman."

Caiaphas lifted one of his silver eyebrows. "You were present in the market?"

"We were and can testify to the events."

"Then speak on."

"Pharisee Saul's accusations are unfounded. This woman was not trying to gather a crowd. She was merely sharing stories."

Saul moved to place himself between Caiaphas and the men. "Stories told to incite civil disobedience."

Caiaphas warned him with a glare before

addressing the man, "Were the woman's claims intentionally false or rebellious?"

"I don't believe so." The man turned to the others with him who voiced their agreement.

Caiaphas templed his fingers to his lips and beat out a rhythm against his mouth for several moments before returning his hands to his lap. "It seems the charges are unfounded. The woman is free to go."

Salome let out a deep sigh as the guards released their hold on her arms.

"However." Caiaphas held up his finger. "Let this be a warning to you, Salome bat Joseph. I do not want to see you in this chamber again for disturbing the peace we are so desperately trying to maintain. We shall not be as merciful in the future."

Salome hung her head in both defeat and exhaustion.

CHAPTER 5

Sabbath morning dawned on Salome as she stood in the priest's kitchen. Though the seventh day Adonai created was often a wonderful opportunity to rest and enjoy time with family, Salome's soul was anything but at rest. Her arrest two days ago had put a strain between her and her family and stolen her sleep.

She grabbed a day-old loaf, some of Miriam's olive oil, and a jar of brined olives. The widow sent these gifts as a gesture to ease her guilt over what happened in the market. Salome set them on the low table. James requested their family gather for a simple meal to break their nighttime fast so he could speak to them privately. Salome guessed she would be the topic of the conversation.

Zipporah and Ria joined her in the kitchen, though there was little the women could do under the day's restrictions. Their task was to prepare provisions for the household, including the disciples and Priest Theodotos, who would break their fast together in the upper room.

Moges appeared in the kitchen, but spoke nothing more than a few instructions to the two female servants then quickly retreated to ensure the rest of the house remained in order.

Even the household steward's silence toward her felt like a millstone around Salome's neck. How far had news of her arrest traveled?

Setting out a pitcher of freshly drawn water, Salome settled on a pillow near the table and waited. She whispered broken prayers between her tangled thoughts.

James appeared first with Elissa cradling young Joshua. Joseph followed with his new bride, Naavah. Mary, Jude, and Arava arrived shortly behind them.

The siblings quietly took their places around the table, no one daring to speak a word before James allowed.

Salome noticed the empty places among them. She longed for the peaceful presence of Jesus or the encouraging smile of Assia. She'd even take the glare of Lydia, who despised mornings as much as she did being forced to sit in awkwardness. Her sister's quick wit would have broken the tension by now. Even Simon would have spoken up, were he present.

After James led them in a time of prayer, they ate but maintained their stoic quiet. Even Arava only used her hands to eat instead of gesturing with her husband.

The silence was deafening in Salome's ears. She couldn't take any more. "Forgive me, James." Her eyes burned with unshed tears. "I know I've brought disgrace to our family name, but I didn't want to be arrested."

James lifted his head. "Salome—"

"You have to believe me, brother. I was only sharing stories. I wasn't trying to cause problems."

"Salome—"

"I would never do anything to endanger our family or anyone else."

"Salome!" James slammed his fist on the table. "Let me speak."

Salome bit down on her lip and lowered her head.

James adjusted his tunic and settled himself. "Now, the reason I wanted to speak to all of you is to address what happened in the market."

Joseph spoke up, "It wasn't Salome's fault."

"I know that." James gave him a warning glance. "But we receive reports every day of Saul's growing influence over the council. The truth is that all of us have to be more careful. What good can we do the poor and needy if we rot away in shackles?"

Salome kept her gaze downward. What could she do to alleviate her family's fears when she was wrestling with the same ones?

"We are facing a very real threat," James continued.

Salome peered through her hair to see her brother's gaze resting on the face of his sleeping son.

"Every knock on the door feels like a warning."

A loud rattle came from the entryway.

All eyes turned toward James. "I will see who it is. The rest of you finish breaking your fast." He rose and headed toward the front entrance.

Salome looked at the food in front of her. Her stomach hornets protested too much to be covered with the morning's portions.

James returned with Hiram.

Salome caught his eyes on her the moment he passed through the archway.

"Salome." James motioned for her to join them.

She rose to obey, grateful to be excused from eating.

"Hiram has a message for you." James lifted his chin toward the larger man.

"That oil seller lady found me in the market yesterday." Hiram's voice was even but guarded.

"Miriam."

"Right. Her." Hiram cleared his throat. "She wanted me to pass along an invitation to join her and her son at their synagogue today."

Salome turned to James. "She still carries a lot of guilt over what happened. Perhaps I should join her in an attempt to soothe her anguish."

"I'd prefer our family to attend synagogue together."

"I can escort her," Hiram offered. "If she wants to go."

Salome turned to face Hiram, assessing his motives with a silent glare. This man was a mystery. Why would he agree to escort her nearer to another he seemingly deemed competition? Was he trying to push her toward a life with John Mark? She wasn't brave enough to ask the questions aloud, much less hear the answers. She turned back to her brother. "I accept Hiram's offer, if I have your permission. I think it wise to put Miriam at ease. What happened wasn't her fault."

James shared a look between the two of them.

Salome caught his eyebrows raise when his gaze landed on Hiram. Did he question Hiram's motives, too? Or was there more her brother wasn't saying?

"Very well." James clamped his hand on Hiram's shoulder. "You may escort Salome to the synagogue, but I want her back here as soon as it's over, and I want her returned in the same condition."

Salome noticed James' grip tighten on Hiram's shoulder. She almost let loose a giggle at the idea her brother, though well-built from his life as a craftsman, could intimidate a man such as Hiram. Working with stone had built James' strong physique, but it appeared as if Adonai formed Hiram from limestone.

Hiram gave James a simple nod of understanding, but Salome could see the left side of his mouth raise in a lopsided grin. "I'll return her as borrowed."

Great. Salome huffed under her breath. *They've reduced me from a child to a tool passed between workers.*

Hiram inclined his head to her. "I'll wait for you outside."

"No need. I'm ready." Salome kissed James' cheek. "You have my thanks." She moved to follow Hiram.

"You can repay the favor by staying out of trouble today."

She didn't have to turn back to know there was a firm warning plastered on her brother's face. Instead, she kept pace with Hiram. "Did Miriam mention anything else?"

"Not to me." Hiram kept his stride even as they left the house and entered the streets.

Salome lifted the end of her tunic to keep up with him. A dozen questions rushed through her thoughts. Was he angry with her? Was he angry at Miriam for asking him to be a messenger? Was there more going on than she knew? Would Hiram be amiable with John Mark? Did she want the two to clash horns like male goats?

Her whirling queries made her head hurt and kept her lips closed as they made their way to the synagogue.

Hiram remained quiet as well, but Salome wasn't sure if he preferred it that way or if his head spun with the unanswered as well. It wasn't until they came upon the square building that he halted at the entrance. His gaze traveled through the open doorway, but he remained on the outside.

"Problem?" Salome honestly wondered.

He shook his head but kept his gaze fixed. "I know many who attend this synagogue. Not really our sort of people."

The division startled her. What sort of people did

he mean? By attending synagogue on Sabbath, they were at least practicing Jews honoring Adonai with their time. That had to make them some kind of kin to the two of them.

"I know we can't sit on the same side," Hiram finally turned to her, "but stay where I can see you."

His words were as firm as James' and equally demanding. "Of course." She wanted to ease his troubled mind with more, but had nothing to offer.

He ducked inside without further explanation.

Once inside, her first glimpses of the people made it abundantly clear what Hiram meant. The Jews in attendance at this synagogue were some of the wealthiest she'd ever seen. Men and women dressed in their finest tunics. She nearly gagged on the perfumes and oils forming an unseen cloud of clashing scents.

"Salome," Miriam's voice lifted above the din of chattering people.

She turned to find her friend and made her way in that direction.

"I'm so glad you accepted my invitation." Miriam made room beside herself on the lower step to give Salome a place to sit. "I see you brought that handsome tent maker as your escort."

"Hiram's a family friend." Salome found him settling nearby, as close to her as possible and it seemed as far away as he could get from John Mark.

"Didn't I see you the other day in the market?"

Salome lifted her eyes to a group of women behind

Miriam, who also turned in the direction of the question.

"You were the one telling stories," the woman continued.

Salome swallowed the lump rising in her throat and peered down at Miriam, whose cheeks flamed as her gaze returned forward. Salome nodded slowly.

"I thought so." The woman smiled. "Those stories were interesting, but I saw the Temple Guards take you away. Didn't like what you had to say, huh?"

"No, they did not." Salome's empty stomach churned.

"Leave her alone, Rhoda," a woman to her left muttered. "Your father has warned you to make your path straight."

Rhoda huffed and crossed her arms over her chest.

Miriam patted the empty space next to herself.

Salome gladly accepted the invitation to sit and turn her attention to the synagogue leader and away from the interrogating woman.

CHAPTER 6

The air in the synagogue was thick and oppressive, the kind of heat that clung to Salome's skin. She couldn't shake the feeling of the woman staring at her. Wiping dripping sweat from her brow, she attempted to keep her attention on the synagogue leader. The day was waxing and so was her patience for the man's drawn words. She longed for the storytelling voice of her brother. He made Adonai's words sing, a quality she tried to emulate whenever she shared His stories. This rabbi sounded like he was strangling the words to death.

After he finally concluded his message, Rabbi Gershon rose from the bema seat. "As many of you know, there have been some among us who've committed to follow this," he twisted his hand around dismissively, "Jesus of Nazareth." His nose wrinkled. "I want to remind you that anyone who claims this dead blasphemer or his teachings will be aligning themselves with a false Messiah."

Salome's skin crawled listening to the man's railings against her brother. He denounced Jesus' claims and dismissed the miracles performed by Him. She had met many whom her brother had healed, and she knew that no one—lame, deaf, or blind—would choose to revert to their former conditions. The hand of Adonai, wrapped in a craftsman's covering, had touched them.

John Mark rose from his place among the men. "You are the one who blasphemes, Rabbi Gershon."

Salome craned to see the young man.

"Jesus is Messiah!" Red climbed up the sides of John Mark's face. "He is the Way we must follow."

"Silence!" Gershon whirled to face John Mark. "You sit down this moment."

"I will not." John Mark squared his shoulders, looking twice his age. "Jesus is Messiah. Anyone who denies Him is the blasphemer."

"Young man," Rabbi Gershon stepped to the edge of the bema, "I will give you one last chance to sit down and remain silent, or I will make an example of you."

Salome's insides tore. She, too, wanted to shout the truth about Jesus, but the threat of punishment kept her lips sealed. Lowering her head, she peered at Miriam. The mother kept her gaze fixed on her son.

"I cannot be silent." John Mark stood firm. "Jesus is Messiah. He is the Anointed One of Adonai."

Gershon nodded to the men near John Mark. "Bring him forward."

Several men grabbed John Mark's arms and dragged him down the stone steps toward Gershon.

"Since you've refused to recant your blasphemous claims, you must endure the consequences." He nodded to the men. "I will not have you speak such defilement in my synagogue."

The men pulled John Mark toward one of the stone pillars. They stripped off his tunic, exposing his back, and bound his hands to the pillar.

Gasps lifted around the room.

Salome's heart pounded. She knew what would come next, and she was helpless to stop it. Miriam whimpered beside her but remained as still as a statue. She reached to grip the mother's hand, comforting her and herself at the same time.

One man handed Rabbi Gershon a long, braided whip.

"Repent!" Gershon's voice boomed, sending a shiver through Salome. "For the Lord's wrath will come upon those who stray!"

Salome's stomach twisted. She heard the murmurs of the onlookers, their whispers like a swarm of locusts, hungry for the spectacle of punishment.

As the rabbi brandished the leather whip, Salome's heart raced like a wild animal desperate to escape. *Don't!* The weight of fear clamped down on her.

They brought forth a scroll and unrolled it.

Gershon raised the whip high, his muscles coiled like a snake. Salome's breath hitched as the leather sliced through the air with a crack that echoed off the stone walls. John Mark cried out, a sound that tore through her, wrapping around her heart like a deadly serpent.

She clenched her fist, nails digging into her palm,

torn between her instinct to protect and the paralyzing fear of retribution. *Please! Someone stop this!*

The words of Moses poured from the reader's mouth, "'If you are not careful to do all the words of this law that are written in this book, that you may fear this glorious and awesome name, the Lord your God, then the Lord will bring on you and your offspring extraordinary afflictions, afflictions severe and lasting, and sicknesses grievous and lasting.'"

Rabbi Gershon lifted the whip again, loosing another blow on John Mark.

This time, he clamped down on his lower lip.

The reader continued, "'And he will bring upon you again all the diseases of Egypt, of which you were afraid, and they shall cling to you. Every sickness also and every affliction that is not recorded in the book of this law, the Lord will bring upon you, until you are destroyed. Whereas you were as numerous as the stars of heaven, you shall be left few in number, because you did not obey the voice of the Lord your God. And as the Lord took delight in doing you good and multiplying you, so the Lord will take delight in bringing ruin upon you and destroying you. And you shall be plucked off the land that you are entering to take possession of it.'"

As the rabbi raised the whip to strike another blow, something inside Salome shattered. "Stop! You can't do this!" Her words spilled out before she could think, her body moving on its own, driven by a force greater than her fear.

The crowd turned their hungry attention toward her.

Gershon's gaze snapped to her, his face a mask of fury. "This is not your place, woman! Sit down!"

Salome's heartbeat thundered in her ears, drowning out the warnings in her head. She took a step forward. "He follows the ways of Adonai! This punishment is unjust!"

Murmurs echoed all around her.

Gershon's nostrils flared, rage etched into his features. "Sit down or you will join him."

"Please! Don't hurt him anymore!" She shouted, her heart racing as she rushed toward John Mark, desperation propelling her forward.

The rabbi lifted the whip again, and in that moment, everything slowed. Salome stepped directly in front of John Mark, her body shaking. "You can't do this!"

Gershon's whip came down, striking her shoulder with a force that sent a jolt of pain through her whole body. The sting was immediate and felt like a fiery serpent bite. She gasped, falling back against John Mark. Stars exploded behind her eyes as she fought to regain her footing, the world tilted dangerously sideways.

A collective gasp raced through the crowd as many fled their seats in a panicked uproar.

Salome glanced up at John Mark, whose eyes

widened in horror, his fear for her seeming to overshadow his own suffering.

"Salome!" Hiram's cry sounded over the chaos. He pushed through the scattering multitude, reaching her just as she swayed. "What have you done?" His hands were warm and steady as he grasped her waist, pulling her away from John Mark. "We need to get you out of here!" His grip was insistent, a mixture of urgency and protectiveness.

She felt his strength, his determination radiating like a shield against the crowd's growing agitation. "No! I can't leave him!" Salome protested, struggling against him, her heart torn. She turned back to John Mark, still bound, his face pale and drawn. His eyes both pleading and apologizing.

Hiram tightened his hold. "Salome, you're hurt. I've got to get you out of here."

As they stumbled through the crowd, Salome felt the weight of her escape bearing down on her. She was leaving John Mark. Guilt twisted in her gut like a knife.

Pushing through the crowded doorway, Salome pleaded, "What if they hurt him worse because of me? I can't just abandon him."

Hiram's eyes, though filled with fierce determination, softened. "There's nothing more you can do. John Mark made his choice. I promised James I'd keep you safe," his breath caught. "He'll never forgive me."

Pain in her shoulder flared, a searing reminder of

her defiance. She would have taken every one of John Mark's lashes if she could. Jesus had taken much more on her behalf.

Hiram led her away from the synagogue, refusing to release his protective hold.

Flashes of John Mark's horror-stricken face lit her mind's eye. How could so many others stand by while he endured punishment for the truth? How could she ever let fear hold her silent again?

Once they arrived at the priest's villa, Hiram relinquished her over to Elissa's care.

Salome winced at her sister-in-law's inspective touch.

"We're going to have to dress that before infection sets in." Elissa slid her gaze to Hiram. "James will want a report on what happened." She flicked her chin to a nearby room. "He's praying in there, but I'm sure Adonai will forgive the interruption."

Hiram slunk toward the room.

Salome wondered if he was an animal that he might have tucked his tail between his legs. The thought almost made her smile, but the sting in her shoulder brought her back to the shameful moment.

Elissa led her to the next room. "Get out of that damaged tunic, and I'll fetch you another." She hurried away.

Salome inspected the rip across her shoulder stained with blood from her gash. Her injury wasn't deep, but it would take time to heal. The unknown number of lashes across John Mark's back set the hairs of her head on end.

Returning, Elissa made quick work of slathering honey on the wound and wrapping it with clean linens. "I'm glad the others are still at the synagogue. I can't imagine the look on your poor ima's face had she seen you like this."

"Why are you back early?"

"Joshua soiled his tunic." She tied the ends of the cloth. "James and I came home to clean him. He's sleeping now."

Salome slipped a fresh tunic over her head and sucked in a breath when she moved her shoulder to adjust it into place. "You're not going to ask me what happened?"

"I don't have to." Elissa gathered her supplies. "I've tended enough whip wounds to put it together for myself." She left.

Salome followed her out, but hesitated at the raised voices coming from the nearby room.

"You promised to protect her," James' voice bordered on panic. "I can't trust her to your protection."

"Please, James," Hiram's words were beyond desperation, "I can take her away from all this, away from Jerusalem, away from Saul and his reach."

Salome leaned closer to the doorway.

"It's not just about Saul." There was silence for a few heartbeats. "I don't want my sister in the middle of this battle. Enough of my family has been scattered to the four winds. I fear for them all, but I won't sacrifice Salome on the altar of your poor decisions."

"My poor decisions? This wasn't me. This was that oil seller and her son."

"Enough." Salome rounded the corner and entered the room. "I won't have you lay blame at the feet of John Mark or Miriam."

James raised a demanding eyebrow. "This isn't your discussion, Salome."

"It certainly is." She folded her arms over her chest, the movement pulled at her injury. "John Mark stood up for the truth. He stood up for Jesus. I stood up for them both."

"While your intentions may have been noble," James stepped closer to her, "I'm afraid your actions did nothing but cause you pain."

She slowly lowered her arms, releasing the tension on her wound. "I still think it was the right thing to do."

"I know you see it that way." James glanced at Hiram. "But we must be careful with our choices." He turned to face her. "All of us."

"Choices?" It was her turn to lift a curious brow at Hiram.

James cleared his throat. "Hiram has made it known his desire to escort you away from Jerusalem."

She didn't move her glare away from Hiram. "Does his desire include a betrothal?"

Hiram lowered his head.

Her cheeks flamed hot. "I see." Thoughts swirled. "I can't leave my family, and I won't run from fear. My brother has given me a calling; I must be obedient to Him above all else."

Hiram lifted his attention. "What are you saying?"

"I'm saying that I will not stop speaking the truth about Jesus. I'm not going to let fear silence me when my brother has given me a voice."

"No matter what it costs you?" The red crawling up the sides of Hiram's neck clashed with the calm in his question.

She swallowed hard. "No matter what it costs me."

CHAPTER 7

Dawning light of the first day of a new week illuminated Salome's steps toward the open tomb. She spent many first days of the week retreating here when the others went to the temple to teach. Today, she was going to share Jesus' stories in Miriam's home, but not before filling her inner well with the peace only her brother offered.

She came to the tomb, its empty mouth filling her with reassurance. Ducking inside the cool inner space, she settled on the slab. "I will be your witness, brother." Closing her eyes, she pictured Jesus' smiling face. "Just keep giving me the words."

The warmth of her brother's presence won out over the chill of the tomb. Steady and reassured, Salome left and made her way to Miriam's house.

Nearing the structure, she heard boisterous sounds of a gathering. The hornets in her stomach returned to their familiar flight pattern. Would this ever get easier?

She paused at the open door. "Greetings to the owner of this house."

"Shalom, Salome." John Mark filled the space. "Ima was worried you weren't coming today. I think she's invited half the city."

The wide grin across his stubbled face added

sincerity to his words. Was the smile for her benefit? Was he hiding the pain of the wounds she knew marred his back? "Forgive me." She lifted her basket. "I was delayed."

He stepped aside to allow her entrance. "Everyone's waiting for you."

Salome entered the stone home; the warm glow of oil lamps and the expectant faces of the people filling every available space enveloped her. The air was thick with the mustiness of too many bodies in too small a space. Though she caught the faint aroma of freshly baked bread contrasting with the dirt and sweat.

John Mark turned to the doorway. "I've got things to tend to in the grove." He adjusted his short work tunic. "Ima and the others are waiting for you. I'll have to hear today's story another time."

A flutter beat like wings in Salome's chest watching him leave. Part of her wanted to pull him inside, knowing if his back hurt more than the dull ache in her shoulder he shouldn't strain himself with labor. His body needed to heal. But it wasn't her place to order him about. She was neither his mother nor his physician. *Be with him, Jesus.*

"Shalom, dear one."

Salome turned to see Miriam with wide open arms. She leaned into the embrace, accepting kisses to both her cheeks, and returned the warm greeting. "Forgive me for keeping everyone waiting."

"Forgotten." Miriam waved her hand around. "I'm

sure these people would wait all day to hear one of your stories."

The familiar buzzing leapt from her midsection to her chest. "Here." She held up the overflowing basket. "My family sends their greetings."

Miriam received the offering, though there were a few moments of hesitation in her stare.

Salome wondered if the woman wanted to ask about her wound. "I'm well," she reassured her.

A sigh fled Miriam's lips with haste. "I'm certainly glad of that."

It was Salome's turn to hesitate. "And John Mark?"

"Well enough." Miriam patted the side of Salome's basket. "I'll start distributing these while you get settled." She nodded to the only vacant space in the room; a beautifully embroidered blue pillow sat empty, waiting.

Salome carefully maneuvered through the crowd, passing greetings as she went. She recognized some of the faces, though most were new. Her gaze landed on one young face in the back of the room.

Among the compacted gathering, Rhoda, the woman from Miriam's synagogue, stood with her back pressed against a wall. She appeared alone, but curiosity painted her beautiful face as she dipped her head in a slight greeting. Salome returned the gesture before continuing toward her seat.

Settling on the lush pillow, Salome made herself comfortable and looked around the room. A quiet hush fell over the people. In the silent moment, she lifted an earnest prayer. *Help me be Your witness.*

Miriam appeared before her and held out a piece of bread already dipped in olive oil. Salome graciously received it and waited for the blessing before devouring the simple provision. The bread was coarse and dry on her tongue, but the rich oil gave it life and flavor. She prayed the bite would satisfy her stomach hornets enough to allow her to speak.

Her thoughts cleared, and a single story burst on to the stage of her mind. She wasn't sure if it was an answer to her prayer or the remnants of her conflicting conversations with James and Hiram. Either way, it was a story worth sharing, and the people were eager to hear.

Clearing her throat, she began, "Jesus explained the kingdom of heaven will be like ten virgins who took their lamps and went to meet the bridegroom. Five of them were foolish, and five were wise." Her eyes swept over the people. "For when the foolish took their lamps, they took no oil with them, but the wise took flasks of oil with their lamps. As the bridegroom was delayed, they all became drowsy and slept."

Her eyes landed on a little girl hiding in the folds of her mother's tunic. Bright eyes shimmered beneath unruly dark curls. Salome tilted her head to the side, pretending to sleep by making a light snoring noise. The little one giggled.

Salome lifted her head. "But at midnight there was

a cry, 'Here is the bridegroom! Come out to meet him.' Then all those virgins rose and trimmed their lamps." She moved her hands in front of her as if trimming unseen lamps.

"And the foolish said to the wise, 'Give us some of your oil, for our lamps are going out.'" She put her fists on her hips, imitating her older sister Lydia.

"But the wise answered, saying, 'Since there will not be enough for us and for you, go rather to the sellers and buy for yourselves.'" She slowly eased her arms to her lap, overly conscious of her still healing injury. "And while they were going to buy, the bridegroom came, and those who were ready went in with him to the marriage feast, and the door was shut." She paused, finding the face of the girl. Her little mouth hung open in a wondrous gap.

"Afterward the other virgins came also, saying, 'Lord, lord, open to us.' But he answered, 'Truly, I say to you, I do not know you.' Watch therefore, for you know neither the day nor the hour."

In the quiet moment that hung after Salome's last word, her stomach hornets buzzed their displeasure. People would have questions about the story, and she never seemed to have enough answers.

Instead of voices of curiosity, the next sound Salome heard was screaming.

People scattered in every direction, tripping over each other and clamoring for the doors.

Salome rose on watery legs to search for the source

of the commotion, but the press of frightened individuals obscured her view. A shrieking sound of an injured child caused her to turn. The little girl whose attention she'd held during the story lay on the floor, curled up and holding her hand. Streaks of tears ran down her pink cheeks.

Pushing to get to the girl, Salome reached for her just as a large hand clasped around her wrist. The iron grip sent pain shooting up her arm. She twisted to face the flaming eyes of Saul of Tarsus.

"Arrest this one." Saul threw her into the open arms of a Temple Guard. "See she doesn't get away." He turned to snatch another fleeing person.

Salome thudded against the broad chest of the guard, her shoulder screaming in pain.

He clasped her firmly, yet created space between their bodies as he dragged her from the room.

Twisting, Salome searched for the girl. "Please let me get her to her mother. She'll be trampled."

The guard held his tongue as he continued pulling her toward the door.

"Please." She twisted and turned in his grasp, fighting the agony the motions caused in her shoulder. "I beg you, have mercy." Writhing, she escaped his grip only long enough to set eyes on the little girl.

In a flash, her mother scooped the girl into her arms and disappeared back into the chaos.

Salome held her buzzing chest. *Praise Adonai.*

A heavy object collided against the side of her head,

causing her vision to dim and her knees to hit the floor. The tight grip of the Temple guard returned, sending wave after wave of pangs up her arm. Her body turned to liquid in his grasp as he hauled her out of the house.

Bird calls and fluttering leaves filled the air around her, drowned out by the turmoil pouring from the house.

Saul shouted orders, "I want this house cleared."

Dust stirred behind people running through the garden and carts fleeing with whoever could escape.

The guard holding Salome hesitated in front of another larger man. She glanced up into the eyes of the other guard. He didn't even acknowledge her. The first guard forced Salome's arms out while the other wrapped a thick rope around her wrists and tied them together in an intricate knot.

With a last tug to ensure security, the rope bit into Salome's flesh. She sucked air through her teeth at the sting.

"Secure her to the others." The second guard moved to bind the next person.

Salome's guard shoved her to the line forming near the other guards. He tied her to a woman who stood with downcast eyes.

Every part of Salome wanted to offer words of comfort to the frightened woman, but none came. She searched the line of people. Men and women, people she was just starting to care for, stood surrounded by Temple guards bound and faced with unknown futures.

She looked down at her own restraints as hot tears burned her eyes. *I should have listened to Hiram.* Streams flowed down her dusty cheeks as the pain in her head and shoulder pounded.

The concerned glare of Hiram danced in her vision. Why hadn't she yielded to his warnings and kept her mouth shut?

At the call of the lead guard, the line began their march through the garden.

Birds fluttered from branch to branch, riled by the disturbance. Hues of greens brushed against the bright blue sky above Salome as if the olive trees were waving her off on a journey. She craned her head in every direction, searching for signs of John Mark and Miriam, but didn't see them anywhere. Perhaps they escaped Saul's clutches.

Her sandals slapped the packed earth along the path as they left the grove and entered the Kidron valley. What was James going to say when he found out what happened to her?

Several more questions tumbled through her mind as they approached the wide steps leading to the Muster Gate. Each one brought her closer to the question she wasn't ready to face. What would be her own fate?

Temple guards led them through the Temple complex. Burning incense mingled with the songs of David. Worshippers glared at them as the guards dragged them through the crowds.

As Salome kept her eyes averted, guards pushed her through the colonnades and under a set of arches. She stole a glance over her shoulder at the sky before the dim engulfed her.

Barely keeping her feet under her, Salome stumbled along. Step after step led her under the Temple. Each one reminded her of the prophet Jonah sinking deeper into the waves after being tossed overboard. She entered her own Sheol, wondering how long she would remain in its deathly grasp. She prayed it would only be the same three days Jonah spent in the great fish's stomach and the same time Jesus spent in the borrowed tomb.

When they finally reached the bottom step, a foul odor tickled her nose. It was the scent of waste and decay unlike any she'd experienced before. She resisted the urge to hold her breath, hoping to grow accustomed to the scent quicker.

A group of guards waited for her there. They removed the ropes around her wrists. She breathed a sigh of relief as the rough material released its grip on her. The reprieve lasted only moments as they replaced the ropes with heavy iron shackles that caused her arms to bob as she fought against their burden. She imagined massive vines of seaweed wrapping around Jonah as they dragged him to Sheol. In this dungeon, there would be no great fish to swim by and rescue her.

Securing the lock on her chains, the guard in front

of her nodded to the other and pointed down the long corridor.

Salome's guard turned her around and marched her away.

They stopped at a large metal door where he unlocked the door and shoved her inside.

Stumbling forward into the dark, Salome caught herself with one knee and her shackled hands.

An intense groan accompanied the loud clang of the door returning to its place behind her along with a single click of the lock.

Salome lifted her gaze to see several sets of eyes on her. Men and women of various ages and conditions huddled around the small room. Some she had seen in Miriam's house; others were complete strangers. She lifted herself to stand before them.

Several turned away. Others allowed tears to flow freely.

Moving slowly, she found a space near one of the three stone walls that imprisoned them. She pressed her back against the wall and slid to her bottom. She placed her arms in her lap, her wrists already protesting the weight of the chains and her shoulder crying out against the additional strain.

In the dim, the sounds of wails lifted all around.

A deep groan grew in Salome's chest. She, too, wanted to cry out, but her pleas came in a different form. "Give thanks to the Lord, for He is good, for His steadfast love endures forever." She lifted her eyes and raised her hands. "Give thanks to the God of gods, for His steadfast love endures forever."

She looked at the people. A few turned in her direction. "Give thanks to the Lord of lords, for His steadfast love endures forever..." She waited for someone to accompany David's song.

"To Him who alone does great wonders," a woman in a corner finished the line.

Salome smiled at her. "For His steadfast love endures forever."

The woman lifted her eyes. "To Him who by understanding made the heavens."

"For His steadfast love endures forever." Salome waited for the woman to continue, but she bowed her head instead.

A heavy silence filled the space.

"To Him who spread out the earth above the waters," a man huddled across from them continued the psalm.

Salome nodded at him. "For His steadfast love endures forever."

He rose to his knees. "To Him who made the great lights."

"For His steadfast love endures forever," Salome chanted the refrain.

He lifted one shackled hand. "The sun to rule over the day."

"For His steadfast love endures forever."

He lifted his other hand. "The moon and stars to

rule over the night."

"For His steadfast love endures forever."

He dropped both hands at once. "To Him who struck down the firstborn of Egypt."

"For His steadfast love endures forever."

"And brought Israel out from among them." He pounded his chest.

"For His steadfast love endures forever."

He held out one hand. "With a strong hand and an outstretched arm."

"For His steadfast love endures forever."

"To Him who divided the Red Sea in two." He parted his hands as far as they would go against the restraints.

"For His steadfast love endures forever."

He wiggled his fingers like legs. "And made Israel pass through the midst of it."

Salome chuckled despite her pain. "For His steadfast love endures forever."

"But overthrew Pharaoh and his host in the Red Sea." He moved his hands like waves.

"For His steadfast love endures forever."

"To Him who led his people through the wilderness."

"For His steadfast love endures forever."

The man stilled. His countenance fell, and he curled back into himself.

Salome looked around, hoping someone else would join them.

An older man lifted his face. "To Him who struck down great kings."

Salome closed her eyes. "For His steadfast love endures forever."

"And killed mighty kings," the man's voice cracked.

Fresh tears fell on Salome's cheeks, and she closed her eyes to breathe in the peace of the refrain. "For His steadfast love endures forever."

"Sihon, king of the Amorites..."

"For His steadfast love endures forever."

"...and Og, king of Bashan..."

"For His steadfast love endures forever."

"...and gave their land as a heritage..."

"For His steadfast love endures forever."

"...a heritage to Israel His servant."

As she opened her mouth, several voices rose to join her, "For His steadfast love endures forever."

Salome opened her eyes to see everyone in the cramped space watching her. "It is He who remembered us in our low estate."

"For His steadfast love endures forever," they chanted together.

She raised her hands, the links clamoring together. "And rescued us from our foes."

"For His steadfast love endures forever."

Salome slowly lowered her arms. "He who gives food to all flesh."

"For His steadfast love endures forever."

"Give thanks to the God of heaven." She put her hands on her chest. "For His steadfast love endures forever."

Again, silence engulfed them, but the voices of praise had stopped the weeping. Salome closed her eyes and rested against the wall. Even the throbbing in her head and shoulder had dulled in the light of worship.

CHAPTER 8

Salome awoke to chains clinking in the darkness and the soft murmur of voices mixing with the distant echo of guards' footsteps. Somewhere water dripped steadily, each drop marking moments in the forgotten place. A putrid stench hit her—rotting waste, sweat, and decay. Scents of mold clung to the damp air, and the sharp tang of rusty iron filled her nose as she shifted her shackled hands.

Something dug at her side, and she twisted to reach into the folds of her tunic. Her fingers brushed something hard. She wrapped her hand around it, retrieving the item.

A small carved lioness stared back at her. The figure was the last one Jesus gave her before he left Nazareth to become a traveling rabbi. She treasured the reminder of his care for her and always kept the object nearby. She turned it over in her hand, examining the well-worn spots where she rubbed the chalkstone over the years.

Jesus called her *guwr* as far back as she could recall. The endearing name had been their shared bond. Growing up without a father placed Jesus as the family's patriarch and Salome's primary source of male affection. She'd been his little lion cub her whole life.

Approaching footsteps and the sound of creaking metal caused Salome to shove the lioness back into her tunic.

"Salome bat Joseph."

She rose and lifted her hand to shield her eyes from the light that blinded her from the guard's torch.

"Step forward."

She quietly obeyed.

"The council is ready to hear your case." He checked her chains and nodded toward a waiting guard.

Salome crossed the threshold of the cell and followed the guard toward the steps. She wondered if Jonah felt like this when the fish spat him onto dry land after three days. She was thankful she'd only spent one night in the belly of Sheol.

Passing through the complex, Salome marched beside her guard toward the Chamber of Hewn Stone. The seventy-one men of the Sanhedrin held her fate in their wrinkled palms. These men possessed the power of freedom or chains, but the Romans had removed their ability to sentence someone to death. Only the foreign rulers could sentence a Jew to their grave.

Warm hues of orange and pink signaled the early start of the day. Smoke from the morning incense offering lifted from the priests' courtyard and painted the sky with a layer of gray. Salome inhaled the musky sweet scent of the special blend known only to the Levites, though she detected hints of myrrh, nard, and cinnamon, among others. It was a welcome reprieve from the night of foul odors in her cell.

Amid the fresh air and light, Salome lifted her eyes to the fading night. Imagining her brother at the right hand of Adonai brought her comfort. Jesus sat as her ultimate Judge no matter the verdict the men in dark robes passed on her.

Inside the Chamber, two groups of older men sat on opposing sides of the semi-circled room. Scribes sat at low tables near the back, scribbling feverishly among stacks of parchments. At the head of the room sat High Priest Joseph ben Caiaphas. His graying brows hung low over tired eyes.

Salome's guard led her to the center of the room and halted before Caiaphas.

The High Priest appraised her with a slow and deliberate glare before directing his attention to the council on his left.

Salome followed his gaze. Nicodemus sat among the others. The Pharisee hung his head, denying her even a comforting glance. With his averted gaze she knew he would not speak on her behalf today. The silence was deafening. He had warned her. Hiram had warned her. James pleaded with her to be careful. Yet here she stood because Jesus' urging for her to speak was stronger than all the voices telling her to remain silent.

Saul stood as the accuser, a fitting place for the man who hurled accusations at her as if they were flaming spears. Blasphemy. Heresy. Unwilling to bend a knee to Caesar. Saul threw one spear after another in her direction.

Salome stood with shoulders squared, not daring even a glance in Saul's direction for fear his penetrating gaze would undo her fragile defenses.

Witnesses came forward. No one heralding her innocence, but many asserting Saul's claims.

Salome had never laid eyes on the men who stood in agreement with Saul. Who were they? What did they have to gain from their testimony?

They spoke of the meeting in Miriam's house and reminded the council of Salome's earlier arrest in the market. They pleaded with Caiaphas to do something with the troublesome Way Followers, including making an example of a woman so bold as to teach about a dead Messiah.

Salome shook her head. Way Followers helped people survive; they weren't harming anyone. She was only sharing resources and hope with the poor and needy. As much as she wanted to raise her voice in her own defense, she couldn't. A woman's words held no weight in this room.

The men continued with event after event, twisting Way Followers' efforts at mercy and teaching with sacrilege and rebellion. Their claims attempted to put their growing numbers in a herd alongside the Zealots.

Salome's throat tightened around a rising lump. Stomach hornets raged, causing her empty midsection to roll. When the men spat her brother's name from their venomous lips, she could take no more. "The very sign Pilate inscribed for my brother's cross proclaimed the truth; Jesus is the King of the Jews. I have no king but Jesus."

"There." Saul held up an open palm. "You've heard the declaration from her own lips. Rome sentenced Jesus to death and crucified him."

Fire burned in Salome's stomach, quenching the hornets. She turned to face her accuser. "I saw Jesus risen."

Saul scoffed. "These rumors are nothing more than empty words used to sway the masses."

"You will all see Him again one day." She threw a glance at Caiaphas. "When you stand before Him in judgment."

Saul took a step towards her. "We do not care to hear more about a dead man who attempted to do away with our laws and bring Gentiles into our flock."

Salome set her full gaze on Saul. "The boulder that sits on your chest is the law of Moses, and men have chiseled more of their own laws upon it. My brother didn't come to destroy the Law." She attempted a step toward Saul, but the guard grasped her arm, sending a jolt through her injured shoulder. "Jesus came to take that boulder off you. He carried your burden and shame with Him to the place of the Skull and to the grave which now sits empty. Your burden, Saul of Tarsus."

Saul leveled an intimidating glare. "You're a fool."

"Then I am a fool for Jesus." She pulled against the guard's grip. "Jesus is Messiah."

"He's dead and buried."

"He is risen! I put my fingers where the Roman nails pierced His flesh."

Saul lifted his gaze over her head to the High Priest. "This woman is clearly mad."

"Enough!" Caiaphas cleared his throat. "We've heard enough."

One of the witnesses stepped forward. "May I add one more thing?"

Caiaphas adjusted his robe. "Yes?"

"We have another piece of information this council might be interested to know."

"Speak it quick."

"We've heard that some of the dead man's followers have fled Jerusalem in order to spread their message to other places."

Salome stole a glance between the man and Saul. She watched the tent maker's hunger for the information burn in his eyes.

Caiaphas waved his hand to dismiss the man. "This council is aware of such claims."

"But is the council aware of where several of them are hiding?"

A boulder landed in Salome's stomach. *No.*

Saul stepped in front of the man. "You have such information?"

"We do."

"Then you must speak it."

The man's lips curled upward. "They've fled to Damascus."

"No!" Salome's scream came out in a shriek.

"High Priest Caiaphas," Saul whirled toward the front and bowed to one knee, "grant me permission to pursue these rebels and bring them back here to be justly punished for their crimes."

Caiaphas glanced from one side of the room to the other before returning his attention to Saul. "Granted."

"No!" Sobs rocked through Salome as she tugged against the guard's hold on her.

"Take this prisoner back to a cell," Caiaphas ordered. "We shall give her more time to consider her claims."

The guard's grip around Salome's arm tightened as he pulled her from the Chamber. Her wails echoed off the stone walls surrounding her as she was once more dragged down to Sheol.

CHAPTER 9

Back in the belly of Sheol, the stench overwhelmed her senses. *How long, oh Lord?*

Guards opened a different door for her and escorted her into a smaller cell than the previous one. Though this cell held just as many people.

She stood in the center of the cramped room. Torch light bled through the cracks around the wooden door, providing eerie streams of light around her. She dropped to her knees and lifted her eyes to the ceiling. "Jesus is King." Tears streamed down her face. "Jesus is Messiah." She tucked her chin to her chest. "Have your way, Adonai."

The people murmured to each other.

"Salome?"

She opened her eyes to see a woman approach her. "Rhoda?" Rising on shaking legs, she did her best to embrace the young woman. "What are you doing in here?" She gazed into the red-rim eyes of the girl she'd seen in Miriam's home. "Why didn't you flee?"

"I tried." Rhoda's words faltered. "There were too many guards. I was pushing to get out the back door when someone caught me." Her eyes misted.

Salome wiped Rhoda's moist cheeks. "We're right where Adonai wants us."

Rhoda's eyes traveled the room. "How can you say that?" She pulled out of Salome's hold and waved her bound arms in an arch. "What kind of God wants us locked away with thieves and murderers for listening to stories?"

"The kind of God that promises to remain with us no matter where we are." Salome stepped closer. "The kind of God that sees us even in Sheol."

Rhoda dropped her hands and let her shoulders roll forward. "El Roi is certainly getting an eye full of our misery."

Salome's chest squeezed. She longed to comfort the woman. She wanted so much to take her into her arms like an ima and calm all her fears. Rhoda's name was fitting; the girl held a certain beauty if one could get past the thorns of the precious rose. "Have you been before the council?"

The younger woman nodded without raising her head. "They had witnesses that saw me in the market and the oil seller's house." She slowly raised her gaze. "They think I'm one of you."

"Are you?"

"I didn't want to be counted among you." Rhoda's eyes widened. "But when I opened my mouth to deny everything, there was this strange warmth that filled my insides. I found myself praising Adonai." She sniffed. "I'm not sure I'm completely convinced, but when I tried to separate myself from the Way Followers, I couldn't. Many of the testimonies are unbelievable, and I still don't understand why Jesus didn't set everything right; why He left us in the same state as when He arrived."

"But?" Salome filled the silence.

"But I confessed Jesus is Messiah, and they threw me in here."

Salome lifted her shackled arms and caught the young woman in a tight hold. "I'm so proud of you, Rhoda. You didn't deny Jesus, and He won't deny you."

"Then He better have a great plan." She struggled against Salome, ducked out of her hold, and put some distance between them. "My bridegroom was supposed to come any day to fetch me." She wiped the length of her face. "Now, he'll marry another. No man will endure this shame." She lifted her chains and shook them.

The truth weighed heavily on Salome in the space between them. She couldn't deny the woman's difficult situation any more than she could deny her own. "I don't know the plans Adonai has for you."

Rhoda scoffed and turned away.

"But Adonai does have a plan for you." Salome looked around at the others sharing their cell. "He knows the plans He has for every one of us."

The sound of something metallic sliding behind Salome caused her to turn toward the door. An opening about halfway down stood gaping like a small mouth.

"Visitor," a guard called out.

Several in the room rushed forward.

"Salome?"

The familiar voice on the other side of the wooden door rang through her like a shofar. "Hiram? What are you doing here?" She leaned down to peer through the slat in the door as the others backed away. The broad man could barely bend enough to look through the opening. She saw mostly his beard, but his unmistakable smell of sweat and leather floated into the room.

"Didn't Jesus tell us to visit those in prison?"

Salome heard beyond his attempt at humor as the burden of his sorrow washed over her. "Hiram, I'm so sorry. I should have listened to you."

"True." He cleared his throat. "But it's my fault."

"Your fault?" Salome hit her knees to peer higher through the opening, desperately trying to meet his eyes. "How is this your fault?"

"I should have protected you from the Slaughterer." Hiram's voice shook. "Even now, I should go relieve Saul of his head."

Salome rested her forehead on the wooden door. "Don't."

"How can you offer him mercy when you're weighed down with the chains he's placed on you?"

Salome heard him spit. She closed her eyes, praying for the right words to soothe her friend. "Because vengeance is not mine. It belongs to Adonai.

His mercy flows through me because Adonai has shown me great mercy."

Silence followed her words. She counted heartbeats, hoping the quiet was the sound of Hiram's wrath ebbing.

"James is afraid you'll end up on a cross like Jesus," Hiram's voice was low and broken.

A shiver ran through Salome. She knew well the Romans saw no distinction between male and female when it came to capital punishment; a prisoner in Rome's eyes was only innocent or guilty.

She breathed a sigh of relief for the measure of assurance she could give Hiram and herself. "I will likely be sentenced by the Sanhedrin. The worst they can do is make sure I never see the light of another day. But they do not hold the threat of a cross over my head. The cross I pick up is the one I choose to carry to follow my brother."

"The Sanhedrin didn't spare Jude and the others, and they won't spare you."

Salome recalled her brother's stripes. Scars marred his back from the three-cord whipping Jude and the disciples endured two years ago after speaking about Jesus in the Temple. She had helped tend their wounds. She'd seen firsthand the result of defying the command of the council to keep silent. Her shoulder throbbed where the rabbi's whip had licked her for defending John Mark. There was no guarantee she wouldn't share in more of the same.

A thudding sound and the wood shaking against her head told her Hiram had struck the other side of the door between them. "Tell me something worthy of praise."

"What?"

She adjusted herself to a seated position against the door. "I need to hear something worthy of praise."

It was another several heartbeats before Hiram answered, "Peter and John have returned from Samaria."

She heard a degree of calm in his voice; it was a good start. "How did they find those who believed from Philip's testimony?"

"They're faring well. Though Peter had a confrontation with that former sorcerer."

"Simon?" Salome remembered Philip's story about the older man who saw others believe in Jesus as Messiah and be baptized. Simon also had been baptized and followed Philip as the disciple performed great miracles among the Samaritans. "What kind of confrontation?"

"Seeing that Peter and John gave Adonai's Spirit to those they touched, the former sorcerer offered them money for the same power."

"He didn't."

Hiram chuckled. "Peter put a curse on him, for his silver to perish along with him."

"Oh, Peter." The face of the feisty fisherman leapt to her mind. He always spoke first and thought second.

"Peter told Simon he needed to repent of his wickedness and ask for forgiveness because Peter could see he wasn't right before Adonai."

"I thought Simon believed Philip's message and put away all that sorcery."

"I guess the truth didn't stick to the slippery sorcerer."

"Well? What happened?"

"Peter claims Simon asked him to pray for him and that none of Peter's curses would come upon him."

"Did he?"

"Peter says he did, but isn't sure if Simon was truly repentant. Time will reveal all."

The stillness that settled between them didn't feel as heavy this time. "And what of Philip? Is he planning to return to Samaria?"

"Philip left yesterday, claiming one of Adonai's messengers came to him and told him to go to Gaza."

Visions of lightning-bright beings flashed through her mind. How wonderful it must be to see one. "Truly?"

"Philip seemed convinced enough to go."

"He will be in my prayers." Salome lifted a short petition for Philip. She heard shuffling on the other side of the door.

"Several of the others haven't returned yet."

Burning rose in her throat. Half her family had been scattered along with several Way Followers. "Hiram, I need to tell you something that you must pass along to James."

"What is it?"

She swallowed the fire burning her throat. "Saul knows Simon is heading for Damascus."

Another pound sent the door quaking. "I've got to go."

Salome heard shuffling. "What are you going to do?"

"Pass along your message." There were more sounds of shuffling. "I'm leaving a satchel of supplies for you with the guard. He better make sure it gets to you."

Salome noted the edge in his voice and imagined Hiram pinning a guard with a threatening glare, even though she couldn't see him. "Thank you, Hiram."

"Don't thank me. The food is from your mother." More shuffling. "That Miriam lady told us what happened."

"Miriam is well?"

"She's not sharing a cell here, if that's what you're asking."

Salome hesitated. "And John Mark?"

Silence.

"Hiram?"

"He's not here either."

Even though his answer was chipped, relief replaced the tightness in her chest. She stood and put her palm on the door. "It was nice to talk to you." She listened to the sound of his retreating footsteps.

Rhoda moved to stand beside her. "Do you think the guards will give you the provisions?"

The sound of a lock opening and the hinges of the door groaning answered.

A guard tossed the bag into the cell and slammed the door shut.

Salome retrieved the satchel and opened it to discover all its contents were missing.

Rhoda's cheeks bloomed red. "Those dirty—"

"Careful," the guard's warning crawled through the slat in the door. "That overbearing Jew only said we had to make sure you got the bag. He didn't say we had to give you what was inside." His laugh was dry and sneering. "Give my compliments to your mother. I can't remember when I've tasted bread so good."

Sliding metal sounds accompanied the slat closing, engulfing the cell in darkness once more.

Salome crushed the satchel against her face and inhaled the lingering scent of her mother's care.

"Filthy guards." Rhoda spat.

Lowering the bag, Salome shrugged. "Perhaps they needed a good meal."

"Needed a good—woman, you must be mad." Rhoda shook her head. "Those savages took your provisions."

"It was only food."

"Food meant for you."

Salome twisted the bag in her hand. "If it were intended for me, I would possess it."

Rhoda shook her shackled hands. "You are one strange woman."

A smile tugged at Salome's lips. How many people counted her brother as strange, too? At least she was in good company.

CHAPTER 10

Days were difficult to mark in the cell. Salome counted bowls of gruel instead. The one that was handed to her this morning was her third. The gruel was cold, as the others had been, and this bowl held even less. Her stomach rumbled its desperation. The water they brought was bitter and stale, coating her throat with filth as she forced it down.

A cellmate scoffed upon receiving his portion. "The only thing I have to season this gruel with is prayer."

Salome's thoughts went immediately to her mother. "My ima always said that a good prayer could season any meager meal."

"Your ima sounds like a fool."

"Watch it," Rhoda warned the man. "You're talking to a sister of the Messiah."

"Forgive me, your highness." The man bowed in a mocking fashion toward Salome. "I didn't know we were in the presence of royalty. Forgive me for not wearing my best tunic for the occasion."

Several of the other occupants chuckled.

Salome's neck and cheeks warmed.

"Don't pay him any attention." Rhoda turned her back to the man. "He's a crusty old fool."

Salome whispered a brief prayer and then lifted the bowl to her lips. The thick, coarse sludge slid across her tongue and down her throat. Handing the bowl back to the guard, her thoughts drifted to her mother's garden in Nazareth. "If I were home right now, my ima would have the perfect herbs to help this go down easier."

The older man across the room sneered. "If you were home right now, you wouldn't be eating this filth."

Salome flinched as if his words had struck her.

Rhoda moved to place herself between Salome and the man. "Was your ima good with plants?"

"She still is." Salome's throat tightened thinking of her mother in the priest's villa. What must she be feeling with her youngest daughter sitting in a cell? "I suppose she had to be."

"What makes you say that?"

"Well, I'm the youngest of eight siblings." Salome rubbed her tongue against her teeth, searching for any last morsel of gruel and helping get the stale taste out of her mouth. "My father died when I was just a baby, so my ima had to stretch every coin in her purse and every herb in her garden."

"Eight children?" Rhoda's dark brows lifted. "And no husband? That must have been rough."

"It was." Salome nodded. "But my five brothers all went to work in the quarry as soon as they could."

"Why didn't your ima remarry?"

Salome hesitated. She never considered the question before. Her mother never indicated a desire to wed another man. Though Salome knew nothing but struggle, her mother provided the best life she could manage. "I don't know." It was an honest answer. "My ima loved my abba. Though I never knew him, by the stories they shared about him, he seemed to be an incredible man. Perhaps she simply couldn't see herself with another." Pieces of stories floated through her mind. "We also lived in a small village. Few men lined up to take on the responsibility of eight extra mouths and a woman who claimed to be impregnated by Adonai."

A woman who sat near them clicked her tongue. "It must've been frustrating to grow in his shadow."

Salome turned towards her. "I don't think chickens would agree with you."

"Chickens?" The woman shook her head. "Who's talking about chickens?"

Salome brought her knees up to her chest. "I simply meant that chicks grow in the shadow of their ima's wings, and they don't think it frustrating. It's the safest place for them."

Rhoda waved off the woman. "What was it like? To grow up with Messiah as your brother?"

Salome lifted her shoulders. "Jesus wasn't Messiah to me until much later. For most of my life, He was simply Jesus, my big brother." She smiled. "I suppose He was the reason life didn't seem so bleak. I didn't care how little food we had or how worn our clothes were. What mattered most was that we were together, and Jesus never let anything happen to us."

Rhoda shifted to sit next to Salome. "But a widowed mother and seven siblings, that's an awful enormous weight to put on a young man's shoulders."

"True." Salome searched her memories. "But Jesus never complained, never even hinted at contempt for His role as our patriarch. He was there, every day, as faithful as the rising sun and steady as the Jordan river." She stretched out her cramped legs. "I think that's one of the reasons He came here."

"What do you mean?"

"I think one reason Adonai sent Jesus was to show us that personal side of Himself." She turned to meet her friend's inquisitive stare. "The relational side, like when He walked in the garden with Adam and Eve."

"Personal side of Adonai?" The old man spit. "Nothing but rubbish talk. Your brother brought nothing but trouble to our people. Even your own family turned their backs on him and look at what it got him." He thrust his hand out, causing his shackles to rattle. "A Roman cross and a tomb."

Salome's lips tugged upward. "A borrowed tomb." The memory of the empty, cold stone table sent a shiver up her arm. "Jesus didn't come to cause trouble or divide our family; He was growing it. We just couldn't see it."

"Well, it doesn't much matter now." He waved

around the cell. "Because we're all stuck in here. Abandoned by Adonai."

"I don't think that's true." Salome lifted a prayer for the man. "Just because bad things happen doesn't mean Adonai has abandoned us. It is our grief that locks us up; that blinds us into believing we are forsaken. Many walk around free yet carry their own chains of grief and sorrow." She rattled her shackles.

"Instead, I marvel at how, when bad things happen, a holy God can humble Himself enough to sit with us in our grief, in the pain, in the darkness of our despair." She looked around at those who shared her cell. "It doesn't matter how many chains they put on our body. If we believe in Messiah, no one can put chains on our soul."

Spiked heels tapped out the sounds of approaching guards. "Salome bat Joseph."

"Looks like you get to see how long those chains will weigh on you." The old man turned away.

Salome rose and presented herself at the open door and breathed another prayer for the man and everyone else occupying her cell as she was led above ground.

Her climb toward the sunlight felt strangely uncomforting. Though the day held similar sounds of worship in the temple and similar scents of morning offerings, Salome's insides quaked with unease. Something was different.

The Temple guard forced her to the Chamber of Hewn Stone and toward her fate.

Passing through the doors and pushed toward the center of the room, Salome eyed the two groups of men on either side of her. Many looked as if they were still sleeping, with heavy eyelids and scowls fixed on their faces.

Sounds of shuffling parchment stirred behind her, and she turned to see both scribes making notes of the morning's proceedings.

"Salome bat Joseph."

High Priest Caiaphas' call fetched her attention, and she set her eyes forward.

"We gave you time to consider your words." He folded his hands in his lap. "We've provided the same to tamper any emotions that may cloud our judgment as the law instructs."

Salome flicked a gaze to both sides of the room. Something was missing. Her focus landed on Nicodemus, who adjusted uncomfortably on the bottom stone step.

"Salome bat Joseph, you've been accused of false teachings and subversion." Caiaphas templed his fingers to his lips. "We've heard ample testimony condemning you of such. But we will give you one last opportunity. Renounce your claims and stop your teachings, and we will allow you to return to your life."

All the attention in the room focused on Salome.

She wet her dry lips. This was her moment. She could recant, return to Theodotos' villa, and resume being simply a bearer of provisions for widows. No one but the men in this chamber would know her choice.

Her eyes slid closed. *No.* Her brother sat enthroned above and, though He knew her intentions, He'd also set a blaze in her soul the day that fiery tongue licked her head. She could no more refuse to speak of Jesus than she could stop breathing.

She opened her eyes and set a firm glare on Caiaphas. "Jesus is Messiah who came to save not only our people but all people."

Several men on both sides of the room hissed or covered their ears.

"Salome bat Joseph." Her name sounded sharp on the High Priest's tongue. "If you do not renounce these claims and stop teaching that Jesus of Nazareth is Messiah, you will be declared guilty and sentenced to imprisonment."

She took a deep breath, allowing the flames in her midsection to lick away the fear attempting to drown it out. "I am but a filthy rag wrung out for my brother and my Lord. If Adonai does that with me sitting in a cell—" she let out a heavy sigh, "—then so be it."

Caiaphas cleared his throat. "Then I find Salome bat Joseph guilty of treason, and she shall be turned over. Let Rome deal with her as they handled her brother." The High Priest dismissed her with a wave.

"Jesus is the King of the Jews!" Salome lifted her voice as she stumbled beside the guard. "I have no king but Jesus!"

The Temple guard pulled her from the Chamber

and back through the complex, down the stairs, and toward the corridor. They opened another door and threw Salome into an even smaller cell. The sound of the lock settling into place sounded so final that it made her weep.

In the dark and damp quiet of her prison, Salome lifted her wet face toward the ceiling. "I have no king but Jesus." She closed her eyes, imagining her brother in all His glory, seated on the throne in the third heavens. "Jesus is King."

Time passed in the darkness, though without the sun or a Roman water clock it was hard to tell how long. The door swung open enough for someone to stumble inside and quickly shut again like a mouth.

Salome stood; her eyes already adjusted to the dim. "Rhoda?"

The woman lifted her shackled hands to wipe at her face. "Well, looks like I have the honor of sharing a cell with the Messiah's sister."

"You didn't recant?" Salome's arms ached to hug the thorny woman.

"I should have, but guess I just wanted to hear more stories." Her gaze lifted around the carved room before settling back on Salome. "And now I'm your captive audience."

"Oh, Rhoda." She threw herself on the woman and did her best to embrace her. "My brother will be so pleased that you've come to be counted as one of His."

"Wonderful." Rhoda patted her arm and pushed

her off. "I suppose they sentenced you to be handed over to Rome as well."

Salome could only nod. Speaking the truth was too difficult to face just yet.

"So, what do we do now?"

A thousand thoughts swirled like a desert storm, but one lifted from the chaos. "We make ourselves useful."

"Useful? I'm the daughter of a wealthy merchant; I don't have any skills. I'm about as useful as jewelry on a pig." She huffed. "I was born to birth more workers, and I don't think Rome is looking for that kind of aid. At least not from a Jewess like me."

"Then I will teach you." Several ideas clung together in the tempest of Salome's mind. "Perhaps we can prove our worth by providing food or medical aid for the soldiers in the fortress."

"I don't want to feed or touch those filthy Gentiles."

"It may be the only way we can survive." The icy vision of a cross sent rolls of nausea through her stomach.

"I don't know how appealing survival is." Rhoda plopped down onto the damp dirt floor. "I'm the first person to be arrested in my family. Don't think they'll welcome me home with open arms. Even if I do survive this."

"I'm not." Salome settled near her, seeking comfort and warmth and to provide what little of both she could. "My brother Jude spent a night in prison. They also held my cousin John in chains years ago for his teachings. I'm not the first, and I have a feeling I will not be the last either."

Rhoda let out a half-hearted chuckle. "I bet Saul loved watching your sentencing."

Saul. The name slammed into Salome's chest. He was missing from the chamber. "Rhoda, was Saul present for your sentencing?"

"No, but I assumed he was there for yours since he seems to have it out for you."

Dread slithered its way up Salome's back. "He's gone to Damascus."

"Damascus? Why would he go there?"

"He's hunting my brother Simon." Salome shivered. "He's in danger, and I can't even warn him. I pray Hiram delivered my message to James in time."

A distant drip filled the silence between them.

"There is one other brother I can tell." Salome lifted pleading eyes. "Rhoda, will you pray with me and ask Jesus to change Saul's intentions?"

"You want me to talk to Messiah and ask Him to change the course of that snake?"

"I know Saul is a viper, but he's also a man. If anyone can get ahold of him and change him, it's Jesus."

CHAPTER 11

Several bowls of burnt gruel later, Salome lay on the dirt floor of the shared cell. Her portions grew smaller with each passing day, and her body ached. The chains weighed heavier on her wrists. After this morning's meal, she could barely lift her head. Her eyes fluttered and begged to remain closed.

The voice that spoke over her all her life rumbled in her soul. *Salome.*

"Jesus," her lips cracked as she whispered His name.

Salome, don't you ever doubt your value, little lion cub. You will be My witness.

Hot tears burned her swollen eyes. "Jesus."

You are no longer guwr, now you are my labiy', my lioness, and you will roar.

A breeze brushed against her cheeks, forcing her eyes open. The strange wind picked at her hair, making it dance. Hints of red shimmered among the dark strains.

Your fire is not quenched, Lioness. The crimson that paints your hair matches the blood of David that runs in your veins. You are a daughter of the royal line. Let your fire be kindled. You merely slumber, Lioness. It's time to wake. It's time to roar.

Bright light filled the room. Salome stared into the growing beam. The shadow of a great lion marched toward her. She lifted her head to take in the vision. As the beast approached her, it opened its mouth and let out a deafening roar.

"Salome."

Rhoda's cry startled her awake.

"Salome." Rhoda shook her shoulder. "There's someone here to see you."

With a groan that came from her bones, Salome lifted herself. "What?"

"A visitor." Rhoda pointed to the open slat in the door.

Digging into her last reserves of strength, Salome dragged herself toward the door and laid her head against it.

"Salome?" Hiram's voice washed over her like a cool wave.

"Hiram?" her voice cracked. She rolled her head enough to peer through the slat. Hiram's eyes were there to greet her, kneeling on the other side of the door.

"You don't sound well." His eyes disappeared from the slat. "Open this door immediately."

"Hiram?" Salome attempted to find him, but he had moved out of her sight.

"I said, 'Open this door!'" Hiram's voice rang out.

There were a few quiet moments before the metal groaned.

Salome slumped to the side as the door gave way under her head.

"Salome." Hiram's muscular arms were under her in a flash. He lifted her to a seated position, holding onto her arms. "What has become of you?"

The smell of dust and sweat clung to Hiram's tunic, mingling with the unmistakable scent of leather. It was a welcome change from the prison stench that lingered in Salome's nose.

Hiram's arms wrapped around her, warm and strong. She pressed her cheek against his tunic, feeling the roughness of the fabric against her skin, grounding her in the moment. His grip was firm, his hands holding her as if he feared she might slip away.

Salome's mouth was dry as she tried to speak, words caught in her throat escaping as a horrid gargle.

Rhoda pressed herself up from her curled position. "They've been limiting our portions."

Hiram looked at the young woman. "Did she get the food I left?"

Rhoda stared into the open doorway. "No."

Salome felt Hiram's grip tighten around her. He mumbled curses under his breath. "Guard!"

A Temple guard appeared at the opening.

Hiram shifted Salome slightly and pulled something from his belt. He threw coins at the guard's feet. "Make sure she gets her full portions."

The guard looked down at Salome. "It won't help."

"I didn't ask for your opinion," Hiram growled.

Collecting the coins, the guard retreated.

Salome looked up at Hiram. "Why are you here?" Her voice didn't sound right in her ears; it sounded strained and too low.

Hiram ignored her and met Rhoda's glare. "How long has she been like this?"

"She's grown worse over the past few days."

"You don't look so good yourself."

"I'll survive." Rhoda laid her head back down. "If Adonai wills it."

Salome jostled as Hiram removed his cloak and laid it over her. The warmth of the extra layer ceased her shivering. He reached to grab something else and suddenly a container was on her lips.

"Drink," Hiram demanded.

The watered wine burned her cracked lips but soothed her dry throat. As soon as the liquid dropped into her stomach, the wine smoothed the rough edges of her discomfort.

Salome heard rustling beside her head.

"Eat this."

She parted her lips to accept whatever food he was offering. Warm flatbread filled her mouth, and she bit into the crisp loaf. Her tongue yielded to the familiar flavor. "Ima's?"

"What else?" Hiram lifted a shoulder and left the loaf near her mouth.

Salome worked the bite and swallowed before taking another. The richness mimicked nuts and mingled with a sweetness that didn't detract from the savory taste of the barley bread. After another bite, she pushed the loaf toward Rhoda.

Hiram moved the bread back to her lips. "I brought this for you."

Salome pushed it again toward her friend. "I can't feast while others starve."

Hiram shook his head. "There never was any sense in arguing with you." He handed the rest of the bread to Rhoda. "As long as you keep eating, you can share what you want."

Salome snuggled against his broad chest and listened to his heart pound like a wonderful drum. "Why are you here?"

"I'm not a dream, if that's what you're asking."

"Well—" she peered up at him "—I have always wanted to see one of Adonai's messengers for myself."

Hiram chuckled.

The sound was so low that Salome almost missed it. She could feel it rumbling in his chest more than hear it.

"I can assure you I'm no divine messenger." He adjusted her in his arms. "But speaking of them, Philip has returned from Gaza. I thought you'd like to hear about his trip."

She nodded against his beard that tickled her face, but she had no strength or desire to brush it away. "Can I have more drink?"

Hiram lifted the skin to her lips.

Salome drained the tempered liquid, allowing the wine to continue its ministration to her weary body. She pushed it toward Rhoda.

Hiram handed it to the woman, who was now partly upright and leaning against the wall.

"My thanks." She accepted the skin and drank her fill.

Salome melted into Hiram's warm hold. "Philip?"

He adjusted her in his arms again and cleared his throat. "When I was here last, I told you Philip shared with us he had seen a messenger that told him to go to Gaza. But he didn't make it there."

Salome shifted to look at his face.

"Settle." He brushed some loose strands of her hair away from her eyes. "I promise it's a good story, though I probably won't tell it as well as you tell them."

She shimmied deeper into his arms and pressed her ear to his chest to add the sounds of his heart beating to his deep voice.

"Philip left Jerusalem for Gaza, but while he was on the road, a chariot came by. In it, there was an Ethiopian eunuch of the queen's court. The man worshipped here in Jerusalem and was returning home when he passed Philip on the road. Philip claims he heard Adonai's Spirit telling him to go near the chariot, so he obeyed."

Hiram's steady voice painted bright images in her mind. She closed her eyes and drank them in as he continued.

"When Philip got closer, he heard the eunuch reading from a scroll of Isaiah. Philip asked the man if he understood what he was reading, but the eunuch said he couldn't understand unless someone helped him."

Salome opened her eyes and looked up at him. "Which portion was the man reading?"

Hiram hesitated. "You know I'm no good at reciting Scripture."

"Please try."

Hiram took a deep breath and let it out with a huff. "'Like a sheep he was led to the slaughter and like a lamb...like a lamb...'"

"'Like a lamb before its shearer is silent,'" Salome finished.

"Which one of us is telling the story?"

Despite the aches in her body, she smiled. "You are."

Hiram took another deep breath. "'Like a sheep he was led to the slaughter and like a lamb before its shearer is silent, so he opens not his mouth. In his humiliation justice was denied him. Who can describe his generation? For his life is taken away from the earth.'"

"Well done." Salome snuggled down again.

Hiram cleared his throat. "As Philip was explaining the passage, the eunuch asked him if Isaiah was speaking about himself or someone else."

Salome's smile rose. "I know who."

"I know you know," Hiram huffed. "But the eunuch didn't. So, Philip got in the chariots and told the man all about Jesus and how He was the one who was led to slaughter like a lamb."

"That's a nice story."

"It's not over yet."

"Oh?"

"As they were traveling along, they passed some water, and the eunuch asked Philip what would prevent him from being baptized."

"Really?"

"He commanded the chariot to halt, and Philip took him down to the water and baptized him."

"Praise You, Adonai," she whispered against Hiram's beard. "Thank you for another brother."

"But that's not all."

Salome peered up at him.

"Philip said when he brought the eunuch out of the water, Adonai's Spirit carried him away, and he found himself in Azotus."

"Azotus? That's almost a four-day journey from Jerusalem."

"Philip said he was quite surprised but started teaching about Jesus in the cities all the way to Caesarea before returning to Jerusalem to inform the others about what happened."

"That really is a good story."

He held her tight. "Not as good as the ones you tell."

CHAPTER 12

Salome lifted herself slowly from Hiram's hold. Though her bones were water, her muscles gained strength from the bread, wine, and encouraging story.

Hiram gently supported her arms. "Take it easy."

"Got anything else in that bag of yours?"

He ruffled through his satchel and produced almonds and dried figs.

She accepted a handful, carefully dropping some into her mouth.

Without prompting, Hiram held out the rest toward Rhoda.

She extended her hand and received a portion with a grateful bow of her head. After pouring as much as she could into her mouth, she spoke around the food, "Now that you're feeling better, Salome, can you tell us a story?"

Hiram held up his palm. "I don't think it's a good idea for her to expel the strength she just gained."

Salome put her hand on Hiram's arm, lowering his hand. "Actually, the passage the Ethiopian man was reading from the scroll of Isaiah reminded me of another." She patted his arm. "The last passage I heard my brother teach in the synagogue in Nazareth."

Rhoda swallowed her mouthful and poured in the

rest. "Will you share it with us?"

Images of Jesus on the bema flooded her soul. "My brother only read the first few lines of the passage and stopped at a very odd place." She adjusted to get more comfortable. "The reading started, 'The Spirit of the Lord God is upon me, because the Lord has anointed me to bring good news to the poor; he has sent me to bind up the brokenhearted, to proclaim liberty to the captives, and the opening of the prison to those who are bound; to proclaim the year of the Lord's favor.' Then Jesus stopped right there, rolled up the scroll, and gave it back to the attendant."

Hiram leaned back against the doorframe. "So?"

"That wasn't the end of the sentence." Salome looked from him to Rhoda. "Jesus stopped because the very next words were, 'and the day of vengeance of our God.' But He didn't say that part."

Rhoda shook her head. "Why not?"

The hornets in Salome's stomach buzzed. Questions were always hard. She never knew if her answers were correct. "I think it's because He wanted people to focus on the 'proclaim the year of the Lord's favor' part and not on the 'vengeance of God' part. One reason Messiah came the way He did was to show that favor and to remind us of the coming vengeance. Adonai is a merciful God. I think that's what Jesus was trying to teach that day."

Rhoda huffed and twisted her chains. "It's too bad Jesus didn't put the focus on the 'opening of the prison to those who are bound' portion."

Salome turned the memory over again in her mind. "I think He did that too." She lifted her shackled arms. "While many of us sit in chains, we are freer now than we have ever been."

It was Hiram's turn to scoff. "How?"

"Our souls are free from the wages of death." Salome kept her focus on Hiram. "By conquering death for us, Jesus freed us from its prison. No matter what happens to our bodies."

The silence that followed gave fodder for the stomach hornets. Salome prayed that Hiram and Rhoda were ruminating on the message and not adding more evidence of her madness.

Rhoda edged closer to them. "Do you know any more of the passage?"

"I do. Would you like to hear more?"

She nodded.

"Let me see." Salome tapped her chin. "The next portion says, 'to comfort all who mourn; to grant to those who mourn in Zion—to give them a beautiful headdress instead of ashes, the oil of gladness instead of mourning, the garment of praise instead of a faint spirit; that they may be called oaks of righteousness, the planting of the Lord, that He may be glorified.'"

Salome looked up at Hiram, who nodded for her to keep going. "Isaiah was reminding the people of all of Adonai's blessings in a time where they could only see the results of their disobedience." She let her gaze fall. "Adonai continued, 'They shall build up the ancient ruins; they shall raise up the former devastations; they shall repair the ruined cities, the devastations of many generations.' It was going to be their duty to restore what had been lost."

She worked to recall the next part. "'Strangers shall stand and tend your flocks; foreigners shall be your plowmen and vinedressers; but you shall be called the priests of the Lord; they shall speak of you as the ministers of our God; you shall eat the wealth of the nations, and in their glory you shall boast. Instead of your shame there shall be a double portion; instead of dishonor they shall rejoice in their lot; therefore in their land they shall possess a double portion; they shall have everlasting joy.'"

The buzzing in her stomach quieted as the words washed over her soul. Fire stirred where the hornets had been. "Even though the people had experienced great chastisement from the Lord, He was promising them future blessings because of His faithfulness to them, despite their unfaithfulness to Him. He says, 'For I the Lord love justice; I hate robbery and wrong; I will faithfully give them their recompense, and I will make an everlasting covenant with them. Their offspring shall be known among the nations, and their descendants in the midst of the peoples; all who see them shall acknowledge them, that they are an offspring the Lord has blessed.'"

Salome whispered a silent prayer as she gazed

between Rhoda and Hiram. "Then Isaiah added his praise to what Adonai had proclaimed. 'I will greatly rejoice in the Lord; my soul shall exult in my God, for he has clothed me with the garments of salvation; he has covered me with the robe of righteousness, as a bridegroom decks himself like a priest with a beautiful headdress, and as a bride adorns herself with her jewels. For as the earth brings forth its sprouts, and as a garden causes what is sown in it to sprout up, so the Lord God will cause righteousness and praise to sprout up before all the nations.' That's why my brother came. Jesus came to dress us in His righteousness, the righteousness of Adonai, and not our own filthy rags."

She turned her attention to Hiram. "No matter where we are, we are brides and bridegrooms of Jesus. He has dressed us for the wedding feast, and we are simply waiting on the invitation to join the feast alongside Father Abraham and the others waiting for us."

Her thoughts drifted to her father. She knew Joseph reclined with Father Abraham and John Mark's father at the banquet table in the presence of Adonai. She prayed for the day she, too, would join the feast.

The beautiful image quickly shifted, and fear doused the fire burning through her. "Hiram, Saul's gone after Simon."

Hiram hung his head. "We know."

"What did James say?"

"James has forbidden everyone from intervening,

except in prayer for Simon."

She struggled to sit up. "Why?"

"He's afraid if we track down Simon, it will only lead Saul right to him."

Conflicting thoughts warred within Salome.

"James is hopeful Ananias will do all he can to hide Simon, but if any of us attempt to intervene, it might risk his safety and our own." Hiram let out a defeated sigh. "Besides, Saul has horses and Temple guards. He has the advantage."

The reasonings were sound, but the ramifications were far from encouraging. Salome pulled herself straight up, strengthened by physical nourishment, and suddenly embarrassed about being so close to a man who was not her own. "How come you've been the only one to visit me? Surely the others would have come."

"They have expressed desires to visit." He slowly raised his head, revealing a wild fire in his eyes. "I have forbidden it."

"Forbidden? But why?"

A dark cloud enveloped the flames in his eyes. "I couldn't protect you from the Slaughterer's trap, but I can keep the others out of it." He rose, his fists balling at his sides. "I should follow that filthy Pharisee and make him pay for every soul he's put in chains."

A guard stepped near the doorway. "Time to go."

Hiram grumbled under his breath. "I will return." He stormed out of the cell.

The large wooden door slammed shut once more, stealing the light and a few measures of hope with it.

Salome rested her head against the wall.

Rhoda scooted closer to her and laid her head on her shoulder. After several moments passed, she asked, "What was Jesus like as a boy?"

"He was the best." Images of the bright smile and deep laughter of Jesus filled Salome's mind. "He's the one who taught me to climb trees."

"You climb?"

"My other brothers would compete to see who could climb the highest." Sounds of her brothers' laughter and their teasing from high branches echoed through her. "James often bested the others, but Simon was often braver. The older he got, the more he tested the limits of trees. Often resulting in rough falls."

"Your poor mother."

"She often had her hands full with Simon." She looked sideways at Rhoda. "He's only a few years older than me, so my mother was grateful when I came along. She hoped another daughter would be more docile."

"Was she right?"

Salome rested her head on her friend's head. "I probably would have been had I stayed inside more with my older sisters, Assia and Lydia. But their constant bickering sent me chasing after my brothers as often as I could. James, Joseph, Jude, and Simon didn't like me tagging along so much. They'd often climb trees to get away from me and then teased me about not being able to reach them."

"Sounds right for brothers."

"Until one day when Jesus discovered them teasing me. The next morning, he woke me up and walked me out to an old sycamore near our home. He spent all day teaching me to climb."

"How'd that go?"

"I fell so many times that I couldn't sit down for days afterward."

Rhoda chuckled.

"But I made it all the way to the top." She smiled, thinking about the moment. "Jesus climbed up behind me, and we sat at the top of that tree, taking in the setting sun. The sky was a beautiful blend of oranges and pinks. I'd never seen the sky from that height before. It was like Adonai had painted me my very own fresco to mark my triumph."

"Sounds lovely."

"The best part was the pride on my brother's face." She recalled Jesus' smile that lit up his eyes. "He shared in my victory and beamed with joy."

"He sounds like a great big brother."

"He's the best." Salome chuckled. "And the next time my brothers raced up the trees to flee from me, I followed them. They couldn't believe it. I still remember Jesus bent over laughing at the look of shock on their faces when I climbed higher than any of them. To this day, I can still climb higher. But the boys don't climb much anymore. I wanted to try climbing the olive trees in Miriam's…" Her playful thoughts turned gray. "Miriam. I'm worried about her and John Mark. I hope Saul has lost his taste for them."

The silence was heavy between them.

It was Rhoda who finally broke it. "Do you ever wish your brother wasn't Messiah?"

Salome stared at her friend but had no words.

"You know, so you would still have him in your life."

Salome thought back to the moment she shared with Jesus that day she learned to climb. "No." She remembered the day the fiery tongue from the heavens touched her head. "My brother might be gone, but He left pieces of Himself behind in us. That's far better. I wish I had my brother back in my life, but for everyone else to have a part of Him in their lives; that's worth the sacrifice."

Rhoda was quiet for a long time. "I have a piece of Him too?"

"A piece that no one can take from you."

Clanging metal and the groan of the cell door opening startled them both.

"Up!" a temple guard shouted.

Salome did her best to rise, but her legs wobbled as if made of water. Tremors went through her as she stepped toward the opening.

"Move it!" The guard barked and shoved Salome out of the cell. "You too." He snatched Rhoda and pushed her into Salome.

Salome fought to keep herself on her feet. "Where are you taking us?"

"I've got orders to take you both to the Antonia Fortress. Rome awaits."

CHAPTER 13

Pain relentlessly accosted Salome in the cell she shared with Rhoda and two others. The small chamber could barely accommodate one comfortably.

Over the past several months, Rome increased its hospitality by often selecting one or more of them at a time to be removed from the cramped quarters. Though the occasions outside the cell were far from envied. Guards ran their shackles through hewn places in the ceiling, leaving them to hang by their arms. Or, in Salome's case, having her whole body stretched uncomfortably as she dangled on the tips of her toes.

In some cells, guards shackled prisoners' feet, so they could not lie down completely. Beatings were frequent. Open wounds festered, and infections spread from lying in the filth on the floor. However, prisoners often preferred that to the salt baths.

Lice feasted on Salome's scalp while fleas partook of the rest of her body. She endured the pests' bites far better than the rats that nibbled on her during the moments she could sleep. Their sharp fangs clipped and tore worse than the multiple small bites inflicted on her by the crawling insects that infested her hair and hid under her tunic.

Every space in the prison was cold, no matter the season above ground. Salome and Rhoda took to sleeping in hugging positions just to share their body warmth and slept often to preserve their energy.

Though unable to separate days, Salome knew the rainy season was upon them. Repeated shofar blasts not only heralded the Feast of Trumpets in the nearby Temple, but the sounds caused the Fortress walls to vibrate. The deep, haunting calls from the ram's horn reverberated with such intensity, it was as if the stones themselves longed to add their praise.

In a rare opportunity of only her and Rhoda occupying the cell, Salome curled onto her side to doze. Her teeth chattered as she clung to Rhoda, who also curled up in the filth. Salome counted shofar blasts until she ran out of numbers. The last ones in each set lasted for as long as the man blowing the horn could hold the note.

Suddenly, a jolt of pain startled her awake. A large rat feasted on her toes. She kicked it away, but the beast refused to be swayed. He returned with a vengeance, clawing at her leg. She kicked it again, but he was adamant.

Out of nowhere, a blur of gray pounced onto the rat, striking a blow that knocked the vile creature flat on its side. The sleek form covered the vermin.

Salome heard ripping and tearing as she gazed upon her champion.

There, in the middle of the cell, hunched a gray cat

with dark spots that blended into stripes in some places. The feline happily feasted on his meal. When he finished, he set to work cleaning his paws and face.

Salome noticed a strip of leather around his neck. On it was a perfectly formed Roman seal. The red reminded her of the broken seal on her brother's tomb.

"Where did you come from?" She reached for the cat.

"Careful," Rhoda warned, stirring from the commotion. "I wouldn't touch it."

"Why?" Salome pulled her hand back. "Is he dangerous?"

"If you cause him harm, he will be. See that seal?" Rhoda pointed to the strip of leather. "That protection extends to the highest levels for that creature."

"Why would Rome protect a cat?"

"They've formed a partnership. The cats feast freely on the rodents that would otherwise eat the soldiers' grains and leather gear. In exchange for their service, Rome provides the cats with protection. If you cause harm or death to one of them, intentional or not, you will be executed." Rhoda glared at the cat.

Finished with its grooming, the feline pattered toward Salome, its full belly swinging with the movement.

"Shalom." Salome pillowed her hands under her head in an attempt not to touch the protected Roman.

Settling on his backside, the cat stared at her, flicking its tail from side to side behind him.

"Thank you for your service."

He lifted his nose toward her, his tiny nostrils flaring.

"Forgive my unpleasant odor." She glanced down. "I'm unable to bathe in this place."

Rising slowly, he stepped closer to her. In a flash, he flipped himself over, pressing his body against her leg.

Salome froze, unsure of what to do.

Making himself comfortable, the cat stretched his long, sleek body out against her.

With his head near hers, Salome could read the markings on his seal. "Maximus, under protection by Caesar." She hummed. "Maximus? Well, it's a pleasure to meet you. I'm Salome bat Joseph."

Maximus twisted his body and nuzzled against her as if they'd been friends all their lives.

It took everything in Salome to keep her hands where they were instead of reaching to pet the cat. "At least you're not as scary as some Romans I've met." A shiver went through her.

The jingle of metal sent the cat fleeing from the cell.

Salome looked up to see one guard standing on the other side of the bars. He stood tall and imposing, an imposing figure over her. Something in his profile struck a chord inside her. She was sure she'd seen him before, but not as one of the regular guards.

"Don't touch the cats." He didn't bother looking

at her. "Or do, if you'd like your stay to be shortened. Though I'm not sure you're ready to meet your god." He marched away with heavy footsteps.

"I've already met my God," Salome whispered. "I'll be ready when He decides I'm done." She watched him leave; something in his odd gait nagged at her. The young soldier seemed so familiar, and yet she couldn't place his face.

Rhoda rolled over. "That Salvus is as nasty as a jujube thorn."

Salvus. His name brought a flood of memories. The sweat-soaked nights, the fever, the prayers she whispered over him. Salome rose to a seated position and pressed her face against the cold iron bars. "Of course. Salvus."

"You know him?" Rhoda edged closer.

Salome searched the corridor as best she could, but could not find him. "My family cared for him after a viper bit him a few harvests ago." She settled back. "My sisters and I helped tend his injury while my brothers tried to mend the internal one." She lay down in the mire next to Rhoda's warmth. "With a midwife's help, we aided the healing of his physical wound, but my brothers were unsuccessful in their task."

Rhoda scoffed. "Maybe you weren't as successful as you hoped. I think some of that venom worked its way into his soul."

"How did you know him?"

"Last time they strung me up." She rubbed her

shackled wrists. "I heard one of the other guards speaking to him. That's how I learned about the cats, too." She tucked her arms under her chin. "It seems Salvus wasn't living up to Rome's standards for a soldier. They reassigned him to the Fortress as guardian of the cats. His last chance to prove himself worthy, or they'll exile him. Or worse."

Salome rolled over to put her thin nose near Rhoda's. "I think we found an open door to our survival."

"What are you talking about?"

"It might take some work." Salome's thoughts rushed ahead. "But I think Adonai brought Salvus here to help us."

"Help us?" Rhoda shook her head. "I'm telling you, that man is full of poison. He spits venom like he's a viper."

"Don't worry, Rhoda." Salome closed her eyes. "Adonai knows how to deal with snakes."

CHAPTER 14

Salome stirred at the sound of Salvus' odd gait crossing in front of her cell. For days, she'd observed his rotations and memorized the rhythm of his steps. "I see the leg healed."

The young soldier halted mid-step and slowly peered over his shoulder at her.

Rolling onto her back, she glanced up at the stone ceiling. "Joseph told us you took off before giving your wound a chance to finish healing." She dared a peek at him and watched realization overshadow his unease.

"Works well enough." He reached toward his thigh but shook out his hand instead. "I had to report back to my unit, or I was going to find a worse fate than a deathbed."

She knew enough of the Romans to understand. "To die without honor would be a terrible fate for a soldier."

"What does a Jewess know of honor?" He spat.

"Oh, not much." She returned her gaze to the stone above her. "Not much at all. For a Roman, it's honor you seek to sustain you through the next life. For us Jews, it's peace."

"Peace?" He scoffed. "Peace makes people lazy and

dull."

"Perhaps." She rose and leaned into the bars separating them. "But the quest for honor often leaves a trail of blood and death."

He pressed his face near her. "If that's what it takes."

"Is that what it'll take for you to gain enough honor to enjoy your next life, Salvus?"

He pounded his fist on the bars.

The sudden sound and rattling caused Salome to take a step back.

"Keep my name and my honor out of your mouth." He marched away.

Salome peered through the bars, watching him disappear into the darkness.

Rhoda yawned. "I hope that was part of the plan."

Twisting her mouth, Salome huffed at her. "At least I got him talking. And I think he remembers me."

"That might not be the blessing you think it is."

"I'm sure Adonai has a plan for this." She glanced back at the darkness. "I just need to work with Him."

"More praying?" Rhoda yawned again.

Salome sat with her back to the wall. "More praying."

It was only days later when Salome heard an answer to her prayers. Raised voices echoed through the corridor, but she could only catch a word here and there.

Rhoda shivered against her arm. "Wonder what

they're shouting about now."

Salome strained to listen. "It doesn't sound like prisoners. It sounds like the guards. Something to do with the grain, but I can't make out anything else."

"Salvus is in charge of the grain." Rhoda fought to control her shaking. "It's part of his duty as a cat guardian."

Lifting a silent plea, Salome stretched toward the bars. "I wonder if something's happened."

Heavy footsteps heading in their direction suddenly replaced the shouts. Salome knew Salvus was coming. "Pretend to sleep," she whispered to Rhoda.

She peered up at her with a raised brow.

"Please?" Salome squeezed her arm and felt the places where the girl's former wealthy diet was wearing off. "He might speak openly if he thinks no one else is listening."

Rhoda sighed but closed her eyes, laid her head back against the wall, and turned away.

Salvus' hobnailed sandals beat against the stone floor with haste.

As he passed her cell, Salome could almost see the tension rolling off his muscles. "Something wrong?"

He whirled in her direction like a sandstorm. His face red, his eyes wild.

Salome prayed for the right words to calm the raging beast of a man. "I heard the shouting."

"Would you like to do some shouting of your own?" He extracted keys from his belt and unlocked her cell.

Gripping her arm like a bite, she refused to let out a yelp, knowing his anger was only directed toward her because he couldn't release it on the person he wanted.

Salvus yanked her through the opening and slammed the bars on Rhoda, who charged the door. Securing the lock, he dragged Salome away.

She stumbled to keep up. "I can help."

Her declaration caught him off guard, and he hesitated. "You know nothing."

"I know I can help." She stared into his wild, dark eyes.

His nostrils flared. "No one but the gods can help me." He continued their trek.

Reaching a place nearby, he unlatched one of her wrist shackles only long enough to string the chain through a hollowed spot in the ceiling and returned the clasp to its former place.

Salome's shoulders burned as her arms hung heavy against the irons above her head. Her toes danced on the cold stone under her as she attempted to keep upright. "Salvus, please let me help you."

He worked quietly to ensure her chains were secure and marched away.

Hanging her head, she whispered, "More praying."

Sometime later, Salvus returned. He silently unchained her wrist.

The lack of weight caused Salome's free arm to drop heavily at her side and her body to crumble toward the floor. She hit the cool stone hard, pulling the chain from the ceiling and causing it to crash beside her.

Salvus snatched the iron and yanked her up to her knees. He secured her wrist with the shackle and chuckled. "Shame you didn't let out a few screams."

She slowly lifted her head. "My offer to help still stands."

"Unlike yourself." He wrenched the chain around his hand, forcing her to her feet. "I told you; I don't need help from a prisoner."

She held his gaze. "But you do need help."

His jaw worked back and forth.

"It's the grain."

He pulled her up and close to himself. "What do you know?"

"Nothing," she eked out her response against the pain in her arms. "I heard you and another guard shouting about it."

He kept a hard stare on her.

"My family helped you return to duty, Salvus. Trust me enough to bear your struggle."

"And what would you know about trust? Trust is a weakness." He huffed. "You're here because you trusted the wrong people."

"I'm here because I trusted my God more than people."

For a long moment, they stared at each other. Then Salvus broke the silence with a sharp exhale.

"The grain supply is running lower faster than I can estimate." He eased her down slightly.

The cold floor met her bare feet. "Rats?"

"I considered that, but the cats are doing their job well." He glanced around. "Some sacks show signs of tampering, and not by animals." He raised an eyebrow at her. "I've been doing what I can to cut the rations, but I think someone is sabotaging my efforts."

"Let me help."

"How?"

"Assign me to kitchen duties."

He shook his head.

"At least until you figure out who is behind the theft," she hurried to add. "I grew up in a poor family; my mother taught me a lot that could be useful."

"I remember your mother's bread." Salvus' eyes raced down her form until they met her face once more. "Step out of line, and you'll answer to me. Because if you betray me..." He let the warning hang in the air.

Salome's experience told her there were plenty of ways he could fulfill the unspoken threat.

CHAPTER 15

Instead of returning her to her cell, Salvus escorted Salome in the opposite direction. She breathed a quick prayer of thanks that her silent requests seemed to be granted.

Winding their way through several corridors, Salome's head spun. How did the soldiers keep track of where they were in this underground prison?

As the echoes of clanging armor and prisoner groans eased, the overwhelming smell of something burning overtook all of Salome's senses.

Salvus led her to a small kitchen somewhere deep in the prison. The area was not much bigger than the cell she shared with Rhoda. Searching the space, she noticed an open fire that appeared raging, yet it was the first time in a long time she'd been so close to flames. Its warmth called to her and frightened her all in the same moment. A low table was close and held only a few items. She took careful note of what was missing entirely, anything resembling a sharp blade. The Romans were brutal, but they certainly weren't stupid.

"Up!"

Salvus kicked something in the dark that Salome had missed entirely.

Another guard stirred from sleep and bolted to his feet.

"Get that fire under control," Salvus ordered.

The soldier hurried to tamper down the flames.

Salvus whispered curses under his breath. "I see you've been enjoying your liquid rations, Brutus."

"No harm done." Brutus smiled a crooked smile and thrust his chin toward Salome. "You bring something else to keep me warm?"

Despite the heat emanating from the fire, Salome shivered.

"Not this one." Salvus led Salome toward the man. "I'm assigning her to assist you," his tone was sharp and edged. "Only to assist you in meal preparations."

"I think those cats have scratched out your humor, Salvus." Brutus chuckled. "You used to be fun."

"Have fun on your own time. When you're on duty, keep your focus."

Brutus slammed his fist against his breastplate and lifted his arm out toward Salvus in a mocking gesture.

"I may not be your commander, Brutus, but I am in charge when it comes to the rations." He motioned to the stack in the corner.

Several spotted cats lay about the pile like soldiers guarding their keep.

"You and those flea carriers." Brutus scratched his beard.

"They have more honor than you." Salvus reached for the nearest cat, scratched behind his ear, then turned to leave.

Salome cleared her throat and raised her arms.

Salvus glared at her. "I suppose you need your hands unbound to work."

Brutus put himself between the two of them. "You're gonna trust this woman?"

"It will be your duty to keep her in line." Salvus moved to unlatch Salome's wrist shackles.

Lifting the iron weights, her arms nearly sang their freedom.

Salvus gathered the chains. "She has received a warning, but I believe she'll be an asset to you." With that, he turned to leave.

Salome watched his steps. The soldier did much to hide his slightly awkward stride. She turned to face Brutus.

He folded his arms over his chest. "Whatever deal he made you, he'll betray you."

She tilted her head.

"Mark my words." He pointed to a grinding stone in the corner. "Get to work." Settling back to his place, he sat down and laid his head against the stone wall.

Salome moved toward the grinding stone near the grain. The cats hissed and growled with her movements.

"Guess Salvus forgot to tell his precious cats that you'd be working for 'em." Brutus chuckled under his breath and sipped from the skin at his side. "The first few scratches sting, but you get used to them." He closed his eyes.

Salome's mouth fell on one side. She knelt to inspect the grinding stones. One flat stone sat inside a large bowl. Another sat on top of it with a notch carved out on one side, a hole dug out of the center, and a piece of wood lay across it. She lifted the top stone and noticed some grains already laying between the rocks. Long brown kernels of spelt were partially ground. She never worked with the grain before, but knew it to be favored among the Romans.

She returned the top slab to its position and inserted the piece of wood into the notch. With a few practice turns, she got the rhythm and pressure needed to move the stone. The sound of grinding brought tears and memories. How many days had she spent grinding? How many of them had she wished away instead of treasuring?

Wiping her face on her sleeve, she reached for more kernels.

The nearest cat swatted at her, catching the top of her hand with his claw.

"Ouch!" She recoiled.

Brutus laughed. "Told ya."

"How am I supposed to grind if they won't let me handle the spelt?" She wiped at the red seeping from her scratch.

"Endure." He lifted his shoulder. "Isn't that what you Jews do best?"

Salome turned toward the collection of cats. Many

of them eyed her right back while some turned away, indifferent toward her. The large gray feline closest to her warned her with another swipe as she attempted to reach for the stack again. Only this time, Salome was faster and caught a few kernels without being struck.

"Lucky snag," Brutus offered and laid his head back. "We'll see how many times you can beat the cat."

"What do I do after I grind?"

"That'll take you a while. Spelt's far coarser than the grains you're used to." He closed his eyes. "When you're done, water's in the pitcher, pot's near the fire. Equal parts spelt and water. Let it boil till it thickens."

"That's it?" She looked around the room. "Spelt and water?"

"There's fat on the table." He pointed.

"Milk would be better."

"You can always try to milk the cats." He laughed. "The fat provided doesn't last long, as it's shared with the pests."

Salome watched a hoard of flies buzz around the table, landing here and there on the pieces of fat. She sighed and poured the kernels from her hand into the hole in the stone and picked up the piece of wood.

While grinding, she hummed a low tune, one of her favorites of King David. She soon heard snoring from Brutus, and even the cats seemed calmer under her melody. Though she still endured many scrapes from them while attempting to secure grain.

CHAPTER 16

As much as she hated to admit it, Brutus was right. Spelt took much longer to grind than the wheat and barley she was used to grinding. The prolonged task of grinding spelt freed her mind to pray and praise. While she preferred the warm kitchen to her cramped cell, she worried for Rhoda left alone to freeze without her warmth and the other prisoners who waited on the *puls* to fill their empty bellies.

After her labor at the grinding stones, she followed the simple instructions to deposit equal parts ground spelt and water into the pot near the fire. With the spoon provided, she gave the mixture a few good stirs and left it to come to a boil.

Searching the table, she discovered rotting pieces of animal fat covered with flies, another spoon, and stacks of bowls. All the tools available to feed the prisoners under their charge. She eyed the cooking mixture that was simmering and thought of all the simple meals her mother provided from equally humble provisions.

She longed to forage among her mother's courtyard in Nazareth. There, it would have been easy to find something to enhance the meager meal. Even their ornery goat would have supplied milk to add richness and flavor. Here, in a damp underground prison, there was nothing but prayer.

Battling the flies for the scraps of fat proved ultimately unfruitful. What pieces she could rescue would endanger the health of anyone consuming the gruel. Defeated, she pushed the remains to a corner of the table and allowed the flies to feast.

The bubbling puls spit at the fire, causing it to hiss. Salome controlled the flames as much as she was able. Using a long stick, she spread out the coals to help the fire settle.

Brutus' snoring and the cats' watchful gazes seasoned her work.

"Up! You mangy dog."

Salome spun around to see Salvus hovering over Brutus.

The drowsy man stumbled to his feet. "That woman's a siren."

"Get up, Brutus." Salvus shook his head. "You know sirens sing sailors to their deaths. You're no sailor."

"I'm telling you," Brutus rubbed his face, "that woman cast a spell on me."

"I'll no sooner believe that than when I see hogs overhead." Salvus moved toward the fire, though slightly impeded by several cats winding their way through his legs. "And why is this puls sitting unattended?" He grabbed the spoon from the table and quickly stirred the lumpy mess in the pot.

"Brutus said to let it boil."

"Brutus doesn't know his head from a tree stump." Salvus continued stirring. "The trick to thick and smooth puls is to stir it constantly. If you just let it boil, it will be nothing but lumps." He glared over his shoulder at Brutus. "Like the ones I'm going to give you if you don't put down that skin that I know has more wine than water."

Capping his skin, Brutus cleared his throat. "What does it matter if that stuff is lumpy or smooth? We're just supposed to feed these animals, nothing more."

"The thicker the puls, the more we can stretch it." Salvus scratched the head of the largest cat sitting on top of the stacks of grain sacks nearby. He tapped the spoon on the side of the pot and held it out to Salome. "Stir."

She reached to obey, but he held onto the spoon and turned it sideways to inspect the back of her hand. Her eyes darted to the cats, but she said nothing.

Salvus let out a frustrated huff. He released his grip on the spoon and stepped closer to her. Reaching for something in his belt, he produced a piece of cloth. He held out his hand.

Unsure of his unspoken request, Salome laid the spoon in his open hand.

He let loose another rough exhale and shoved the spoon into her other hand. Gripping her wrist, he held up her injured hand. With the cloth, he tightly wrapped her scrapes and secured it with a knot. "There."

She pulled the bandage to her chest. "My thanks."

"It's not for aid," he kept his voice low. "It holds my scent. It'll help them trust you." He shifted his gaze to the cats.

Salome nodded as her cheeks warmed. She misinterpreted his actions, but she caught something different in his glance. "Anything to help with the other animal?" Her eyes slowly moved toward Brutus.

"Nothing I've found."

There it was again. Almost light in his eyes, almost humor in his tone. Both snubbed out as quickly as an oil lamp in a downpour. She moved toward the fire. "I'll stir the puls."

"Don't bother." He sighed. "That pot is ruined. The prisoners will be grateful to have something warm. You can do better with the next batch." He nodded to Brutus. "Let's get this mess distributed."

Using some cloths from his belt, Brutus carefully removed the pot from the flames.

"Grab the bowls." Salvus motioned with his chin.

Salome collected the stack of bowls.

"On me." Salvus marched out of the kitchen area.

Working their way through the corridor, Salome stayed between the two soldiers. Salvus led the way, opening and closing cells. Brutus carried the large pot and portioned the lumpy puls into the bowls Salome held up.

Several prisoners gave ungrateful glances when the mixture plopped into the bowls.

Salome could not meet their disgruntled eyes.

The two soldiers marched her through the prison, feeding each prisoner.

In one crowded cell, Salome discovered a man curled up who refused to rise and receive his daily portion. She reached for him, her fingers touching chilled skin. She gasped, and the man groaned.

"Thought him dead?" Salvus clicked his tongue. "Won't be much longer."

Salome looked at the man beside him. "What's his name?"

"Samuel," he answered, drowning his bowl of puls.

Salome knelt beside the older man. "Samuel, you must eat, or you will die."

He coughed a dry and short cough in reply.

She held up a bowl to Brutus.

He hesitated. "More merciful to let him die."

She shoved the bowl toward the soldier until he reluctantly added a small scoop. Holding the bowl to Samuel's lips, she begged, "Please eat."

Samuel opened to her, but the puls dribbled out the sides of his mouth and onto the ground.

Brutus whispered curses under his breath.

With pleas to Adonai, Salome tried again, but the man choked on the gruel and began a raging coughing fit. She set down the stack of bowls in her other hands and rose to remove her cloak.

Salvus gripped her arm. "What are you doing?"

"Giving up my cloak." She motioned down to Samuel. "This man is freezing."

"You want to cause a riot?" He glanced at the others sharing the cell. "These people will slit your throat for such a prize."

She yanked her arm out of his grasp and continued to remove her outer cloak. Tenderly, she wrapped Samuel in the warm material.

His cough settled, and he closed his eyes.

Though the chill of the underground tore at her, the warmth in her soul fought against it.

The man next to Samuel leaned closer to her. "Can I have it when he dies?"

Waves of horror and shock rushed through her. The man's request was honest and earnest. She looked at Samuel, who appeared old enough to be her father yet resembled a swaddled newborn.

"I'll make sure he keeps it," the man continued. "But when he breathes his last, can I have it?"

Tears burned her eyes, and all she could do was nod and retrieve the bowls. She left the cell and heard the groan of the door as it settled into place.

CHAPTER 17

They spent the rest of the time silently distributing the bowls of food. Only the sounds of their sandals against the stone floors added to the drip of distant water and the groans of prisoners and cell doors.

Salome saw every kind of suffering; cold, malnourishment, festering wounds, fevers. If the elements weren't bad enough, the guards provided torture to ensure anguish in this place.

By the time they returned to the kitchen, Salome could no longer keep her tears from falling.

"Save your pity." Salvus scratched and petted the cats that welcomed him. "Every prisoner is serving their due punishment."

"But we could provide them with aid." Salome couldn't help her pleas. "With the same provisions used to make puls, I can bake bread."

"We don't provide medical aid to prisoners." Salvus folded his arms across his broad chest. "And bread would require more grain and more time simply to give empty hope." He shook his head. "We need to distribute the water rations next."

Salome stepped back. "We must see them all again?"

"If you're not fit for this duty—"

She held up her hand. "I am." Her stomach flipped. "I just wasn't ready for the horror I'd face."

He grabbed a large pitcher. "You'll get used to it, or I'll relieve you of this duty."

Several thoughts collided in her mind. "May I ask one request?"

He hesitated.

"As we are providing the water rations, can I have time to pray with those who are sick or injured?"

"You are certainly cruel."

"Cruel?"

"First, you speak of medical aid and bread. Now, you wish to give more false hope by praying over these people?"

Fire tore at her throat. "May I remind you that your widow neighbor's care and prayers, motivated by her faith in her Messiah, and my family's medical treatment and prayers, saved your life."

"That's—"

"And, had it not been for my sister, Assia, who went to help that widow because it is what our brother called us to do, or her fight to have our midwife friend come to your aid, you would also not be standing here."

His lips formed a thin line, and his jaw muscles flinched.

She waited for his response, praying it would come in the form of words and not torture.

"No aid. No bread." He adjusted the large pitcher.

"But you may pray with them." He snatched a stone cup. "And don't give away any more of your provisions. I don't need them fighting any worse than they already do."

She nodded her agreement.

"Brutus, you stay here and start cleaning out that pot and those bowls." Salvus gestured toward the mess. "She's going to help me get this water passed around, and then I'm putting her back in her cell for the day."

"You mean I gotta clean, and she gets off?" Brutus wagged his finger at Salome.

"She didn't sleep on duty." Salvus leveled a challenging stare at the soldier, who matched his height and build. "Twice."

Brutus let loose a string of curses as he turned toward his task.

Salvus marched out of the kitchen. "Keep up."

Hurrying after him, Salome kept to his back as they traveled the twists and turns of the underground.

In each cell, Salome filled the stone cup and allowed each prisoner to drink their portion. Whenever she encountered someone who was sick or suffering, she stopped to pray. Some prisoners accepted the offer of prayer with their water. Others groaned their displeasure or simply huffed at her.

Cell after cell, she spoke at least one prayer, even if there was no apparent physical need or reception. When she reached a cell in which she recognized some Way Followers, she asked them to join her in the prayer. Several prisoners gathered around and spoke their prayers aloud. Salome wept at the sounds of bold petitions lifting from these fellow followers.

"What is going on here?"

Salome turned to see a guard approach them.

"Commander Ursus." Salvus stood to attention and saluted his superior. "This prisoner is assisting me with the daily water rations."

Ursus appraised Salome with a glance and then the rest of the prisoners. "This is no temple, so why are you standing watch for a prayer gathering?"

Ducking her head, heat rose up the sides of Salome's neck. What had she forced Salvus into?

"Better having them pray than riot." Salvus kept his body straight and his eyes forward. "Sir."

Ursus once more assessed the group and Salome. "There is such a thing as being too lenient with prisoners, Salvus." He stepped closer to the guard. "Remember that and how thin your favor within this unit is already."

"I understand, sir." Salvus pulled Salome from the cell and secured the lock behind her.

"Finish your task and report to me when you're through." Commander Ursus marched away.

Salvus led Salome in silence to the last few cells, then returned shackles to her wrists and deposited her in the space she shared with Rhoda.

When the bars groaned and the lock clicked behind her, Salome sunk into the mire next to Rhoda.

The younger woman scooted closer. "Profitable day?"

Salome slid her eyes to her friend. "Not as much as I hoped."

CHAPTER 18

Salome stirred the bubbling puls while keeping a sharp eye on the flames underneath. Her arm ached, and she switched hands. Salvus' suggestion of constant movement proved to be profitable. The more she stirred, the more the mixture developed into a thick, rich consistency. Her dedication aided with stretching the limited spelt supply, but for some reason, the inventory was coming up shorter and shorter.

Salvus stepped into the kitchen area.

She heard his gait before she turned to face him. Having memorized the sound, she might never forget it.

His movements were tense, and unease shadowed his usual stoic demeanor. He carried a small sack in one hand, his expression as hard as the fortress walls. Something unreadable tempered the usual sharpness in his eyes.

"More grain." He dropped the sack onto the floor with a dull thud, causing some cats to scatter. "Don't waste it."

Salome's gaze flickered to him, then to the sack. Although it wasn't much, it would help ease the strict rationing imposed on the supply. "Thank you."

He grunted in response, his attention already shifting to the cats weaving through his legs. He reached down to scratch behind one's ear before straightening. "If you're going to smuggle food, at least be smarter about it."

His accusation stung worse than the cats' claws. "I'm not the one stealing from you." Salome stepped back, her hands curling around the spoon. "I'm doing my best to stretch these meager rations."

Salvus leaned against the edge of the kitchen table, his arms crossed over his chest. "Someone is stealing." His sharp gaze locked onto her, searching for cracks in her resolve. "I think I have a fairly good idea who. I just can't prove it. Yet."

Salome swallowed hard, trying to steady her breathing as she released the tension in her hands. "What will you do when you find out who it is?"

He pushed off the table and began pacing, the spikes of his sandals scraping against the rough stone floor. "It's not my job to be their judge."

She stepped into his path, her chin lifted. "You'd forgive them?"

Salvus stopped, his brow furrowing as he looked at her. "You talk about forgiveness like it's easy," he muttered, his voice heavy with bitterness. "Have you forgiven the ones who put you here?"

Salome faltered, lowering her gaze to the floor. Her fingers caressed the slight lump in her tunic where the lioness statue resided within. "Not yet." She looked up at him again. "But I'm trying. Forgiveness doesn't mean forgetting the pain, it means trusting Adonai to use it."

A bitter laugh escaped his lips. "If your god is so powerful," his voice low and laced with sarcasm, "why doesn't he free you?"

Salome softened, staring into his dark eyes, praying her words could penetrate his unseen walls. "I'm already free."

Her words hung in the air, and Salvus turned his head slightly, appraising her as several emotions flickered across his face. Suddenly, his jaw tightened, and for a moment, she thought he might walk away. Instead, he straightened, and every sign of emotion washed from his countenance.

"You could be as well," she added, her voice trembling but determined.

He let out a sharp breath, his lips twisted into a wry smile. "I think you're forgetting which one of us wears the chains." He gestured toward the shackles that encircled her ankles.

Salome held his gaze, unflinching. "You may not see them, Salvus, but you wear chains, too. Chains of anger, bitterness, and fear that you carry on your soul. But you don't have to carry them."

For a moment, his stoic mask faltered. His eyes flickered with something—doubt, regret, or maybe something deeper. But it was gone as quickly as it came. He shook his head, brushing past her as he grabbed the water jug from the table.

"Don't waste the spelt." He marched out, his footsteps purposefully weightier.

Salome watched him leave; her heart heavy but hopeful. For all his defenses, she knew her words had struck a chord. Whether or not he admitted it, Salvus was wrestling with more than just a grain problem.

Salome returned her focus to the puls and her mind to her prayers.

Brutus' footsteps broke through her concentration. She moved to give him a path toward the pot.

He swayed, attempting to reach for the container. The fire threatened to kiss his skin with a warning lick. He recoiled and wrapped his hands with cloths before trying again. Stepping backward, he swayed once more, nearly dumping the pot.

"Careful." Salome lurched to steady the vessel but didn't grasp the hot metal.

Letting out a string of curses upon her, Brutus pulled it out of her reach. "I know what I'm doing." He adjusted the pot. "Get the bowls and let's go."

She looked around. "Shouldn't we wait for Salvus to return?"

"I'm not wasting my time waiting." Brutus marched away. "He can catch up."

She grabbed the bowls and scurried after him.

When they stopped at the first cell, Salome held up a bowl for Brutus to fill it.

He scooped a small amount.

She glared at him.

"Problem?"

"That's not enough."

"It's plenty." He nodded toward the prisoners. "Go on."

With a huff, she passed the bowl to waiting hands and continued her glares as Brutus barely filled the next one.

While the prisoners slurped down their meager portions, Salome prayed with the sick and asked after those who had endured sickness and torment. She joyfully listened to the reports of healing and praise.

"Let's move," Brutus barked. "Unless you want to stay with them."

Salome hurried out of the cell so he could secure the lock.

At each cell, Brutus' impatience grew until Salome could barely feed everyone.

After locking the last cell, Brutus marched away.

Salome looked down at the large pot he left on the ground. "Aren't you going to carry this back to the kitchen?"

Without even a glance back at her, he yelled, "It's your turn to scrub!"

She stared down at the pot that still contained remnants of puls, and then at the prisoners in the cell next to her. She stooped and filled a bowl. "Here." She passed it through the bars. "Give this to the sick one."

The man glared at her for a moment; his fingers

tightened around the bowl.

"If you obey, I'll give you some too," she promised. "He's sick and in need of nourishment."

He closed his eyes and handed it to the ill man.

Gulping down the few bites, the sick prisoner nodded his gratitude and handed the bowl back to the man.

Salome reached for it.

"If you have more, there is another in here who could use it."

He met her eyes, and she could see a glimmer of something kind. "Of course." She filled the bowl and handed it to him.

This time, he passed it to another man quickly and waited for him to empty it before passing it back through the bars.

She filled it a third time and held it up to him.

He stared at it for a few heartbeats before releasing a long sigh. "I'm sure there are others who could use it more." He hung his head.

"What's your name?"

"Jason."

"Can I pray for you, Jason?"

He lifted his head. "Please?"

She whispered pleas on his behalf and added the two sick prisoners who shared his cell to her prayers. Hurrying to the next, she distributed the bits left in the pot and added her prayers while they ate.

Knowing she had little time before Salvus

discovered her absence, Salome quickly collected the pot and the bowls.

"May your god bless you."

She turned to see Jason pressed against the bars. "He already has."

CHAPTER 19

Straining under the weight of the pot, Salome made her way through the dim corridor toward the kitchen. Her arms ached, and her stomach growled from hours of labor with little to eat.

As she rounded the corner, she froze. There was Brutus, hunched over and stuffing a sack of spelt beneath his cloak.

Her breath caught in her throat. The sight of the powerful guard acting like a common thief sent a jolt of anger through her. "What are you doing?"

Brutus' head snapped up, his eyes narrowing as he closed the distance between them. His expression darkened, but there was a glint of estimation in his eyes. "What does it look like?" He shoved the sack into her hands with surprising force. "Catching our grain thief."

"Me?" She struggled against his grip, her heart racing. "I—"

Before she could finish, heavy footsteps echoed from the opposite direction. Relief and apprehension mingled as Salvus appeared, his expression dark and questioning. "What's going on here?"

Brutus smirked, tightening his grip on Salome's

arm as he turned to face Salvus. "Caught her in the very act." He gestured to the sack now clutched in her trembling hands. "Your little storyteller's been sneaking supplies. And you," he jabbed a finger at Salvus, "have been helping her."

Salome's pulse pounded in her ears. "That's a lie!" She struggled against his hold. "I have taken nothing!"

"Who do you think they'll believe?" Brutus chuckled, his tone dripping with mockery. "A prisoner and a poor excuse for a soldier? Or me, a guard with a spotless record?" He leaned closer to Salvus, his voice lowering to a venomous whisper, "What's one more dead Jew matter to our vast empire?"

Salvus clenched his fists at his sides and fixed his cold, unyielding eyes on Brutus. "Don't try to pin your theft on her."

Brutus laughed darkly, clearly savoring the tension. "Let her take the blame, and I'll cut you in on my profits."

"Profits?" Salvus spat. "You indulge beyond your wage, and you expect prisoners to pay with their starvation?"

Salome's mind raced. Brutus' inability to walk straight most days, the foul stench of wine on his breath, his hours snoring on the floor of the kitchen—it all made sense. He was stealing to fund his vices. Her stomach turned at the thought of how many prisoners had gone hungry, possibly starved to death, because of his thirst.

"Your greed will cost you—" Salvus began, but Brutus raised a hand to cut him off.

"I've heard enough. It doesn't sound like we agree. So, save your speech for the commander. He'll be thrilled to hear about this...betrayal." He turned toward the corridor, signaling two guards who had appeared at the commotion. "Take them both to the commander."

Salome's chest tightened as the guards advanced. Her fingers gripped the sack involuntarily, the rough fabric biting into her palms. "Wait—this isn't—"

"Quiet," Salvus ordered. His eyes met hers, a silent warning flew from them. The tension in his jaw and the flicker of fire in his eyes betrayed his inner turmoil.

Dread coiled in Salome's stomach as the guards seized her arms.

Brutus gestured sharply for Salvus to follow, his smug expression taunting them both.

As they marched toward Commander Ursus' quarters, Brutus fell into step beside Salvus. His smirk widened as he leaned in. "I warned you, didn't I?"

Salvus said nothing, his face a mask of calm. Yet Salome could see the tension in his rigid posture and the whiteness of his knuckles as his hands remained at his sides.

The corridor seemed to stretch endlessly. Flickering torchlight cast long, distorted shadows that danced around them like specters of judgment. Salome's heart thudded in her chest as she whispered a silent prayer. *Adonai, give me strength.*

When they reached the commander's office, Ursus sat behind a wide wooden desk, his icy gaze sweeping over them. Brutus launched into his report with exaggerated conviction, his hand slapping the desk for emphasis. Each word was a dagger, twisting the truth into a weapon.

Ursus steepled his fingers beneath his chin, his expression unreadable as his gaze shifted between them.

"This soldier's been smuggling supplies," Brutus declared, his tone heavy with self-righteousness. "The prisoner was his accomplice."

Ursus leaned forward, his voice low and deliberate, "Do you deny the charges?"

Salvus stepped forward, squaring his shoulders. "No, Sir," he said evenly. "It was my decision. The female prisoner only followed my orders."

Salome's breath caught. Her head snapped toward Salvus, her eyes wide with shock. "That's not—"

"Enough!" the commander barked, his sharp gaze pinning her in place.

She bit down on her bottom lip, sending silent pleas with her eyes to Salvus. The rigid soldier moved his head in the slightest shake that she almost missed had it not been for his wide glare that seemed to scream at her.

Ursus' attention shifted to Salvus. "As for you, soldier, you've betrayed your post and endangered this fortress."

"No!" Salome pulled against the unyielding grasps of the two guards at her sides. "He didn't do anything wrong!"

"Silence!" Ursus' voice echoed off the stone walls as he rose to his feet.

The sound reverberated through her, causing her insides to quake. She whimpered and ceased her struggle.

Turning back to Salvus, he continued, "You'll be reassigned to Philippi immediately. Perhaps they can teach you what honor and duty mean."

Salvus stood motionless, his expression unreadable, though Salome saw the flicker of pain in his eyes.

She whimpered again.

He gave her a brief glance, another slight shake of his head—a warning to remain silent.

Ursus shifted his stony gaze to Salome. "And you…" he lowered himself back to his seat, "…the lash will teach you some respect."

Salome's heart plummeted. Her breath quickened. She fought against the two guards' hold. "Salvus, please."

With a flash of movement, he stepped in front of her, his voice so low it barely reached her ears, "A life for a life. My debt to your family is paid. Give me this honor, that I may have credit in the next life."

Her knees wavered, but she steadied herself, lifting her head despite the burning tears. She glanced into his eyes one last time, his expression a storm of rage and insistence.

Her lips quivered with all the arguments she wanted to say. He couldn't do this. She wasn't worth it. She knew her place was set at Adonai's table but his was not.

Commander Ursus' order broke through the moment, "Take her away."

As the guards' clasps on her arm tightened and pulled, Salome whispered a trembling prayer, "Adonai, watch over him."

CHAPTER 20

"Come, little rebel," Brutus ordered, towering over Salome.

He grabbed her from the other guards. The bite of his grip felt like a viper sting. He dragged her along, his hold sending waves of pain through her worn and weary muscles.

"I warned you." He yanked her hard.

Salome stumbled but steadied herself, straightening her back. "I have done nothing wrong," she protested, though her voice trembled.

"We'll see how long that courage lasts." He shoved her forward.

Her heart pounded recalling the teachings of her brother—His words about strength in weakness, love amidst persecution, and forgiveness in the face of fear.

Snaking their way through the underground, the darkened passage gave way to light as they ascended the steps into the Temple complex. As they reached the courtyard, the sunlight hit Salome like a wave. With her time in the belly of Sheol, she'd forgotten how bright the sun was from its height in the sky.

Brutus marched her toward a crowd gathered around the flogging post. The metal ring embedded in the concrete glimmered in the daylight.

Salome searched the crowd, and her heart sank when she discovered familiar faces among the onlookers. Some of their expressions held a mix of worry and disbelief.

Brutus pulled her toward a raised platform and secured her chains to the ring on the post.

"Stop! Let her go!" someone shouted from the crowd.

Salome recognized the voice and twisted to find the source.

Craning to see through the crowd, John Mark stood, clutching his mother Miriam against his chest.

Salome's chest squeezed. She wanted to run to the two of them and embrace them with words of comfort and encouragement. She was so grateful they were not bound as she was.

"Silence," the overseer's voice bellowed. He nodded toward the guard with the whip.

The soldier unrolled a strap of braided leather.

Salome whispered a prayer of thanksgiving for the measure of mercy found in the absence of shards of bone and metal that were often found at the ends of those tails.

She searched the crowd, hoping to find strength in their gazes. The fear she found mirrored her own. She remembered the only place she could find the strength she would need to endure what was coming her direction. "Jesus is Messiah!" she cried out, her voice ringing with conviction. "He is Savior! You cannot silence the truth!"

The whip cracked against her back, the sting sharp and immediate. Salome gasped, her body jerking involuntarily against the restraints.

People in the crowd murmured, some turning away, others looking on in horror.

Another lash followed, and Salome forced herself to breathe through the pain, to remember that suffering had purpose.

Feeling blood trickle down her back under her tunic, she shouted, "Jesus is Messiah!"

Murmurs spread louder through the crowd.

The next lash sent her to her knees. Spasms raced up her legs as the pain flamed through her back. She clung to the post, gasping for air. She clawed at the short pillar, trying her best to endure. Hot tears raced down her cheeks.

Salome. Jesus' voice rang clear through her like a shofar blast. *You have King David's blood running through your veins. You have My Spirit flaming inside you. Rise!*

She put one foot under herself but faltered. Her knee smacked hard against the marble under her.

Rise, Lioness! Rise and roar!

She set her foot under her again and slowly rose on watery legs.

The soldier stopped, panting and confused.

Salome stood, bloodied and bruised, yet filled with

an unquenchable hope. At that moment, she knew her sacrifice was not in vain. She turned over her shoulder. "Jesus. Is. Messiah." She set eyes on her torturers. "I forgive you."

"Get her out of here!" the overseer ordered.

Two guards unchained Salome and marched her back underground. Instead of returning her to her cell, they escorted her toward the stone bath.

The sight of the watered-down salt caused her back to spasm. She knew what was coming next.

Without even removing her ripped tunic, they lifted her into the basin.

Salome's vision blurred; the raw sting of salt against her torn skin burned like fire with each labored breath.

The soldier who held her down grunted as he pushed her into the coarse grains which had settled to the bottom. Salt seeped into every open wound, amplifying the searing pain until Salome's body trembled violently. The angry welts on her back screamed for relief, but she refused these men the satisfaction of doing so. It was as though the salt carved out a new kind of agony, one that reached deeper than the wounds on her body. The pain was overwhelming, but Salome refused to yield.

Her legs buckled, and she felt herself swallowed by the salty water. Silence engulfed her under the surface, reminding her of the dip in the pool of Siloam on the Feast of Shavuot. The day the fiery tongue licked her head and changed everything. James lowered her into the water, and she rose with an internal fire that often quenched everything else. The fire that attempted to penetrate her body from the salt was no match for the Spirit of her brother that flamed inside her. *What can they do to my body, Jesus, when you hold my soul?*

A low, mocking laugh echoed from one of the guards above her. "This should be enough. Get her up."

They yanked her from the stone bath and set her on her feet.

Salome swayed on shaking legs, saltwater dripping from her entire body.

"Back to her cell?" one guard asked.

It was then Salome lifted her attention and saw Commander Ursus watching the torture.

"No." He held her gaze. "Take her below."

Guards hauled her upright, then roughly dragged her deeper into the prison. She winced, her entire body in agony.

In the darkest part of the prison, the guards halted. They threw a thick rope over the side of an empty cistern and, without ceremony, lowered Salome down.

The bottom came faster than she expected, the force of the descent striking her against the cold, wet ground with a sickening thud. She gasped; the air knocked from her chest, but there was no time to recover. They recalled the rope, abandoning her in the dark.

Salome blinked, adjusting to the dimness of her new surroundings. Darkness like she'd never known embraced her. Suffocating silence and sharp muscle pain were her only companions. She shivered in the coldest place she'd ever been. The cistern felt more like a tomb than a cell.

She recalled the story of Joseph, how his brothers had put him in an empty cistern until they could decide how to rid themselves of his pestering presence. Adonai used that path to eventually raise him to second in command over all Egypt.

Joseph's words to his brothers echoed inside her. *You meant evil against me, but God meant it for good.*

She pulled her legs to her chest and whispered her brother's name, "Jesus, I know you are with me. Even here."

CHAPTER 21

In the cramped space of the cistern cell, Salome curled tightly against the curved wall, her knees pressed to her chest. The cold wet ground beneath her offered little comfort, and the dampness in the air felt like a suffocating blanket, pressing against her skin and seeping into her bones. Every breath felt too shallow as if the walls themselves were closing in on her, each inhalation an effort. She hugged her arms tightly around her knees, trying to keep herself warm, desperately missing Rhoda.

Her whole body throbbed, but the physical pain paled in comparison to the ache in her spirit. She whispered words of Moses and the prophets under her breath, her voice barely audible above the drip of water that echoed in the silence.

Shadows danced from the faint light of a torch far above, flickering across the curved ceiling. A clatter of hobnailed sandals above broke her concentration. Muffled voices followed, growing clearer as they approached the opening.

Salome stiffened; her breath caught in her throat. Her stomach knotted with dread. They were coming for her again. A swirl of uncertainty twisted through her. What would they do to her this time? More torture?

Even in the darkness, her faith flickered within her like a stubborn flame that refused to die. It burned bright against the crushing weight of fear, but the fear was always there, just beneath the surface, threatening to smother her resolve.

The silence that followed was broken with a shouted command, "Bring her up!" Then a thick rope fell and stopped near her head.

She rose on shaking legs, weakened from an unknown number of days in confinement. Grasping the rope, she wrapped it quickly around herself, secured it with a simple knot, and gave it a tug. Her feet lifted from the mire as she was pulled upward.

Near the top, two guards grabbed her arms and yanked her over the sharp edge of the cistern. She didn't resist as they undid her knot and bound her wrists and ankles with shackles. The rusted edges of the metal bit into her skin. She had no strength left for resistance.

There was no warmth or even a hint of compassion from the soldiers, only precision and efficiency. How she longed for the warmth of kindness.

"Pontius Pilate has summoned you," the soldier muttered. His tone was indifferent, but there was a flicker of something in his eyes. Curiosity? Pity? It was gone before she could be sure.

Pilate. The name struck her like a blow. It carried

the weight of Rome's authority, and more than that, it carried memories of her brother's trial. She would stand before the same man who condemned Jesus to death even after declaring Him innocent.

The other soldier shoved her forward, and she staggered, catching herself before she fell. Her feet stumbled as she fought to keep her balance, the weight of the chains dragging her down.

Her heart pounded as she was led through the fortress, her bare feet scraping against the rough stone, up the stairs and into the Temple Complex.

The brightness of the sun assaulted her as she emerged. She squinted, her eyes watering. The sudden transition from dark to light was too much for her senses.

Air outside the cell was thick with the heat of midday, and as they crossed the courtyard, Salome could feel every eye on her. Noises enveloped her: the clink of armor, the barking orders of soldiers, the hum of distant conversations. All around, life went on despite her suffering and the suffering of those underfoot.

Guards marched her to the Stone Pavement. The massive open space was bordered by columns and overlooked by a raised platform where the governor's seat of judgment stood.

Holding up a hand to shield her weary eyes, Salome saw a figure seated on the throne.

Pilate sat draped in the crimson sash of his office.

His face stern, a mask of authority. His eyes, sharp and calculating, flicked to her as she was dragged forward. The sun gleamed off his polished armor, and a faint breeze carried the scent of sweat and incense.

A shiver raced up her legs when her bare feet touched the marble before the platform, still slightly chilly even with the climbing sun. Her chains clinked against the slab as she was forced to her knees by the guards. Her heart raced, and for a moment, fear threatened to overwhelm her. But then she remembered Jesus. The weight of His cross, the scars on His back, the crown of thorns pressed into His brow. If He could endure such suffering, she could endure this. She straightened her back, lifting her chin despite the trembling of her body.

Pilate's voice broke through the thick air, his tone both commanding and dismissive, "Salome, sister of the Nazarene. When they informed me you were occupying one of my cells, I had to see for myself." He leaned forward, studying her. "You've caused quite a stir among your people. Teaching in the streets, defying the orders of the Sanhedrin. Tell me, why do you persist?"

Salome hesitated, her mind racing like an Egyptian stallion. She could feel the familiar buzzing in her stomach, like a thousand hornets stirring inside her. She felt the weight of every eye on her—the soldiers, the onlookers, the officials standing at Pilate's side. The air seemed to close in around her, the eyes of the onlookers bearing down on her like the weight of a thousand stones.

She bowed her head, weariness settling into her bones. Her body felt like iron, as though the weight of her time in captivity had finally caught up with her.

They all wanted her to cower, to deny everything and return to a quiet and obedient life. Hiram's smile flickered in her memories. She could recant and be his.

But the idea of betraying everything she believed in, everything she knew about Jesus, crushed her. How could she deny the One who had given her strength, who had transformed her into a woman of courage? How could she deny her Messiah?

Then she heard it. *Salome.* Jesus' voice, strong and clear, both shook her and strengthened her innards. *You have the blood of a lioness of Judah coursing through your veins. Speak!*

Tears welled in her eyes, blurring her vision, but she lifted her face, her heart swelling with the power of His words. She could do this. She had to do this. She felt defeated, pressed down, and beaten—but not broken.

She took a deep breath, drawing strength from the Spirit that burned within her. "Because Jesus is Messiah," her words came out in a squeak, barely a whisper, but they were enough. Raising her shackled arms, the chains rattling as if to announce her defiance, she wiped tears from her face. "Jesus is the Son of God." Her voice grew stronger, more resolute. "Jesus is the only King of the Jews!"

A murmur rippled through the crowd.

Pilate's lips twitched, almost imperceptibly. Was it amusement? Annoyance? She couldn't tell.

"And for this," he said slowly, "you are willing to die?"

"I am willing to live for it. For my Messiah." Her words hung in the air, bold and unyielding.

Pilate's expression darkened. He gestured to a scribe who stepped forward, unrolled a scroll and read aloud the charges against her: sedition, disturbing the peace, inciting rebellion. Each word felt like a stone added to her burden, yet she refused to bow under the weight.

When the scribe finished, Pilate leaned back in his seat. "The Sanhedrin advise your continued imprisonment until you agree to cease your teaching. They consider you a threat to their authority. Tell me, Salome, are you truly so dangerous?"

Salome met his gaze. "Truth is dangerous to those who deny it."

Pilate's jaw tightened, and for a moment, silence stretched between them. Then he stood, his movements deliberate, and descended the steps to stand before her. He was taller than she expected, his presence imposing. He studied her as one might study a caged animal, curious and detached.

"You remind me of him," he said softly, his voice carrying only to her ears. "Your brother. He, too, stood here, defiant in the face of my power. Do you think your god will rescue you as he did not rescue your brother?"

Salome's throat tightened, but she forced herself to speak. "My brother's death was not a defeat. It was a victory. Through Him, all who believe have life."

Pilate stepped back. "I am not interested in your theology," he said sharply. "What matters is order. Rome cannot tolerate chaos, nor can I." He turned to the guards. "Return her to her cell. She will remain there until she agrees to abandon this...folly."

A boulder sank into Salome's stomach, but she refused to show it. As the guards grabbed her arms, she looked up at Pilate one last time.

"You have the power to imprison my body," she rattled her chains, "but you cannot imprison the truth."

Pilate's expression flinched; his eyes narrowed. "Truth." Another long moment passed in his hesitation. Then he turned to ascend the steps. When he reached the top, he resumed his seat and waved his hand to dismiss them.

The guards hauled her away, the weight of her chains dragging against the ground. As she was led back to the cistern cell, she prayed silently, her heart determined. She would not yield. Truth would endure, even in darkness.

CHAPTER 22

A clang on the metal bars sent shocks through Salome. She woke, fearing where she was. She'd survived a long stretch in the cistern cell, much to the displeasure of the Roman guards. Whether due to pity or simply easier access to torment her, they eventually moved her back to the cramped cell with Rhoda. The passing of time was evident in the thinning frame and hollowed eyes of her friend.

"Visitor," the guard called out with another pound on the iron.

Salome lifted her eyes and smiled at the face she'd not seen in a long time. "Hiram."

"Where's the cloak I gave you?"

"Not even a shalom for your friend?" she teased.

"Where is it, Salome?"

She bit her lower lip and pulled her tattered tunic closer around herself. "I gave it to Samuel."

"It was for you."

"He was dying, Hiram. I couldn't watch him freeze to death."

Hiram gazed around. "Where is he?"

Salome looked down.

"He froze to death anyway, didn't he?"

Tears stung her eyes. She couldn't speak the truth.

Hiram muttered curses under his breath. "How can you hope to survive if you give away the provisions I bring?"

"I've survived this long because it has been Adonai's will." She lifted her chin to meet his wild gaze. "If not..."

Hiram ran a shaking hand through his hair and knelt. He stared at her for several long heartbeats before letting out a long, heavy sigh and pressing himself against the bars.

She adjusted to get as close to him as possible. The warmth of his body called to her. He was like her personal cooking fire.

Rhoda snuggled closer to them, drawn to the extra heat like a moth to a flame.

"Forgive me." Hiram pressed closer. "I didn't come to argue with you."

She nuzzled into the bars, aching to once again hear the gallop of his strong heart. "Tell me a story."

"First, I need to tell you about some things that have happened."

She lifted slightly. "My family?"

"Shalom. Everyone is well." He patted at the air. "It's been a while since I've been able to see you because a lot has happened that has prevented my visits. We've received news from some Way Followers in Samaria. A man there claimed to be Moses returned in the flesh."

Salome's nose wrinkled.

"He started gaining a following and promised he could show them where Moses hid the sacred vessels near Mount Gerizim."

"That's absurd."

"Many believed him." Hiram ran his finger down one of the bars. "The group was on their way to Mount Gerizim to retrieve the vessels when Pilate intervened with a thousand soldiers. Pilate executed the leaders but allowed the others to go free."

Salome gasped.

"It should have ended there, but the Samaritans considered Pilate's actions excessively violent."

"I would say so."

"They claimed the group was unarmed when Pilate's soldiers attacked them, but there are conflicting accounts." Hiram huffed. "The Samaritans appealed to the Syrian governor, Lucius Vitellius."

"Did the governor intervene?"

"Vitellius sent an *epimelete* named Marcellus to relieve Pilate from office."

"Does he have such power?"

"Not officially." Hiram waved his hand around in a circle. "More like one governor giving another a chance to go explain themselves before Rome stepped in. Vitellius strongly suggested Pilate go before Emperor Tiberius concerning the accusations of the Samaritans."

"So, Pilate's gone?"

"Yes, after taking time to get his affairs in order,

Pilate set sail for Rome. Vitellius' first official act was the removal of High Priest Joseph ben Caiaphas."

"Rome is certainly making a habit of disposing our High Priests whenever it suits them." She rested her forehead on the bars. "Adonai decreed that only death could remove a High Priest. With Rome in control, they seem to displace the position as frequently as they do the governor's seat."

"I think that's another reason Pilate complied with Governor Vitellius' suggestion that he go to Rome to plead his case. Pilate's been prefect over Judaea for ten harvests. It was highly unusual for one to hold that position for so long."

"Who's the new High Priest?"

"Jonathan ben Annas." He adjusted to look her in the eyes. "If that change isn't bad enough, there's another that's taken place."

"Oh?"

"Emperor Tiberius is dead."

"I thought you said Pilate went to Rome to speak to him about the Samaritan disruption."

"Pilate was traveling to Rome, but we've recently received word that the emperor has died."

"What happened?"

"As is tradition, Emperor Tiberius took part in the ceremonial games by throwing a javelin. During his throw, he wrenched his shoulder and took to his bed to heal from the injury. He fell ill and lapsed into the sleeping death. His physicians, whom he had forbidden to examine him for decades, discovered he'd been wasting away for some time and declared that he would die by the end of the day."

"What an awful way to die."

"But that's not how he died."

Salome raised a curious brow.

"They sent for his successor, Caligula, and the Praetorian Guard declared their support for him. But Tiberius woke from his sleeping death and asked for food."

"Then what happened?"

"This extraordinary healing confused the Romans, and they weren't sure what to do." Hiram lifted his shoulder. "The following day, the Praetorian commander Marco went into Tiberius' chamber and took the blankets and smothered the emperor until he died."

Salome wrapped her fingers around her throat. "Oh my."

When Caligula became Emperor, he immediately replaced Marcellus with a man named Marullus."

"So, we've had two new prefects and a new emperor, yet nothing has changed except the bodies warming the seats of power?" She leaned her head against the stone wall. "Did you bring me any good news?"

Hiram thought to himself for a few moments. "Peter has agreed to take John Mark on as a scribe. He's teaching the boy to read and write, and they've started to record some of Jesus' teachings."

"That sounds wonderful." Salome lifted a silent prayer for her friend. She'd been thankful he seemed to remain out of Rome's reach. "Any other news?"

"There is one other thing." Hiram's gaze moved past her to Rhoda. "I'm not sure if she will welcome this news."

Salome turned to her friend. "Whatever it is, we can face it together."

Rhoda blinked several times, then nodded. "Go ahead, Hiram. Nothing can be worse than my current circumstance."

"I wish I could agree with you." He hung his head. "I wish even more I didn't have to share this with you."

Salome threaded her fingers through the bars as far as she could to caress his arm. She then leaned against Rhoda. "At your word, Rhoda. We'll weather the storm together."

She silently nodded again.

Hiram let out a heavy sigh. "James received word that your father has died."

Salome felt tremors race through Rhoda as she sobbed. She set her chin on the younger woman's head and prayed for Adonai's comfort.

When Rhoda's wails quieted, Hiram stared at her. "There's more."

Salome stole a glance in his direction. She silently pleaded for his next words to carry a breath of comfort.

He shook his head as if to answer her unspoken

request.

"Adonai has a plan for you, Rhoda." She nuzzled her nose against Rhoda's damp cheeks. "No matter what your path holds."

"Speak quickly, Hiram." Rhoda snuggled against Salome. "Perhaps the rest will lose its sting in the fresh wound of my soul."

"After your father's death, James and the others tried to visit your mother. They wanted to provide her aid as they'd done countless other widows."

Glaring with wide eyes, she spoke softly, "I thank Adonai for His care through their hands."

"They didn't get the chance." Hiram held her gaze.

Salome felt him shake under her touch.

"Your mother left Jerusalem." He moved his focus to Salome. "After some inquiries, James discovered she fled and left her husband's debts to be paid by Rhoda, since she was already in shackles."

"My mother has left me to carry the burden of my father's debt?"

"I'm afraid so." Hiram looked back at her. "Even if you received a pardon today, you'd remain here until your family's debts were settled."

Rhoda crumbled into Salome as fresh wails echoed in the small chamber.

Salome lifted her shackled arms to embrace her and held her tight against her chest, rocking her like a mother with a child. "We will brave the storm together."

CHAPTER 23

Slight taps of small feet scurried past Salome in the dark. She waited a moment, listening for the sound of Maximus to follow. His movements started completely undetectable, but after memorizing the differences in every cats' rhythm, the sound was undeniable. A swoosh of air and the feather-light touch of his paws on the stone floor were the first hints of his presence.

There was a moment of calm, and she knew the rat could smell its hunter. By then, it was too late. The next sound was a sudden thud as Maximus landed perfectly on the rat, executing a lethal blow to the foul creature. What followed in the dark was the sound of the Roman victor enjoying his spoils.

"You make a fine warrior." Salome glanced toward the sound and caught Maximus' shape among the dim. "Though I'm sure you prefer this battlefield to one above ground."

She listened to the sounds of his chomping and tearing. Sounds that first turned her stomach had transformed into relief that another set of rodent teeth would not be feasting on her flesh. The fleas and lice already made her skin their table all too frequently.

"I will never understand why so many of you Romans enjoy the flesh of rodents, but I'm grateful."

When Maximus had his fill of his meal, he sauntered near, his gray belly swaying with his trot. He curled up beside Salome and set to work cleaning his weapons.

"Just like a good soldier," she mused.

After carefully tending his paws and face, Maximus settled his head on his outstretched arms.

Salome felt his vibrations against her leg and smiled. "I'm very thankful for you, Maximus." She hummed as she laid her head against the wall behind her. "'Make a joyful noise to the Lord, all the earth. Serve the Lord with gladness. Come into His presence with singing.'"

She reached down to scratch Maximus between his ears. Something she'd been warned countless times not to do, but the two had developed a bond through her former days in the kitchen. So much so that the cat made a habit of visiting her no matter where she was in the prison. He was a welcomed companion, especially in times like this when she was separated from Rhoda for periods of isolation in the smallest cell in the prison.

"'Know that the Lord, He is God. It is He who made us, and we are His; we are His people, and the sheep of His pasture.'"

Maximus lifted his head as if offended by the mention of sheep.

"Sorry." She giggled and scratched under his chin as an apology.

He stretched out and pressed against her, his

vibrations continuing.

Another melody started in her mind. She hummed along, lifting the words from her lips to her brother seated in the third heaven. "'For You are great and do wondrous things; You alone are God. Teach me Your way, O Lord, that I may walk in Your truth; unite my heart to fear Your name. I give thanks to You, O Lord my God, with my whole heart, and I will glorify Your name forever.'"

The sound of leathered footsteps slapping against stone halted her praise. She counted paces, longing to once more hear the familiar gait of Salvus. Alas, these footsteps were too heavy and deliberate; they belonged to Brutus.

"Quick, Maximus." She nudged the cat. "Better not let him catch you in here."

Maximus stirred and scurried through the bars no bigger than Salome's balled fist. She never understood how the cat's body could morph into an almost liquid form to fit through different openings.

The footsteps halted, and the metal hinges protested as they opened.

Salome lifted her shackled hand to shield her eyes from the torchlight that would follow. Between her fingers, she saw Brutus' broad form illuminated by the firelight, but there was another with him. The man wore no soldier's armor; neither did he resemble Hiram. Curious, she slowly lowered her hand.

Her eyes adjusted to take in the form of the

Pharisee she hadn't seen in a long time.

Saul? Salome rose on shaking legs, using the wall behind her for support. Had his journey of vengeance to Damascus proved fruitful? Had he come to boast after having hunted the rest of her family, friends, and fellow Way Followers?

Saul stepped into the cell, taking up the only available space.

Salome noted his dark robes, the same ones he wore the day he hurled accusations of blasphemy at her. But there was something different about him. Instead of the sneering grin of a prideful Pharisee, Saul's countenance had shifted. When she finally met his eyes, she discovered an intense fire brewing there.

"Shalom, Salome."

She pressed herself against the wall of her tiny cell, fear clawing at her but the strength of her faith fighting back. "Have you come to hear more about Jesus?"

"As a matter of fact," the corners of his mouth slid up, "I wish to discuss that very thing with you." He stepped out of the cell and faced Brutus. "Remove her chains."

With a huff, Brutus moved toward Salome, extending an outstretched key. He inserted it first into the lock of the shackles on her wrists.

The loud click of the rusted lock sang out in the confined space, followed by the crumbling clang of the metal hitting the stone floor.

Salome's arms buoyed at the lack of weight.

Brutus bent and placed the key in the lock on the pair of restraints around her ankles.

Opening its mouth, the lock groaned, and the chains fell to the side.

She lifted her foot and twisted it in a circle. The lack of weight was strange.

Brutus retrieved both sets of shackles before leaving the cell.

Salome rubbed her aching wrists. "I don't understand."

Saul stepped into the doorway. "I had the charges against you dropped. You're free to go."

"Free?" The word felt as foreign on her tongue as her joints felt without shackles.

"Come." He waved her forward. "There is much to tell you."

She looked up at him, searching his face. The fire in his eyes burned hot, but it wasn't the hate-filled flames that had been there before. This fire was different, yet altogether familiar. "You saw Him."

He nodded but placed his finger to his lips.

She shook her head. "This is a story I've got to hear."

"I will very much enjoy telling it to you." He bowed his head and motioned to the corridor. "Shall we?"

She slipped through the door and out into the open space. It felt so wrong to be out of the small cell unbound. Her heart pounded as if at any moment

Brutus would drag her right back to her chains.

Even as they made their way toward the steps that led out of the prison, she could hardly catch her breath. She placed one toe on the first step as the next words of the psalm she'd been singing to Maximus poured over her like a fresh wave. She lifted her eyes and sang, "'For great is Your steadfast love toward me; You have delivered my soul from the depths of Sheol.'"

The first steps up the stairs sent shivers racing up Salome's legs. She reached halfway and hesitated.

"Salome?"

She turned over her shoulder to look at Saul. "How can I just leave the rest of them?"

"I've been able to free some, but they're not all here because of me. Many of them still have crimes for which they must answer."

She hung her head. "Jesus paid the debt I owed to Adonai." She turned around to fully face Saul. "He's paid their debt, too."

"And mine." He glanced up to meet her eyes. "But you've also paid for others."

She dropped her head to one side. "How so?"

"Lydia and Simon."

The faces of her siblings flashed in her mind. "Are they safe?"

"So I'm told."

With a sigh of relief, the weight of Saul's pain crashed into her. "They're the reason your betrothed is dead."

"And I'm the reason Stephen is dead, and why many others endured the torture and shame of being in this place. And worse." A shiver passed over him. "Simon and Lydia had blood on their hands, yet it was you who paid their debt by spending the last three years in a cell."

"Three years?" Her knees turned to water and her vision shifted sideways. "It's been three years?"

"It has." His gaze traveled the walls. "I was surprised as any to discover you were still here. But now it's time for you to leave this place. Adonai has more work for you."

She took a last glance at the corridor behind Saul and nodded. "I know the work He's called me to do." She turned to face the light. "He will give me the strength for my next steps."

CHAPTER 24

Passing through the arches and into the open courtyard of the Temple complex, Salome stopped to bathe in the sunlight. The fresh air was thick with the scent of burning wood and incense from the altar. People flowed around her as if she were a small boat in a busy trading port.

Saul came to stand beside her.

She kept her face toward the daylight. "You promised me a story."

"I did." He chuckled, his gaze toward the low wall that separated the Court of Gentiles from the holier places. "The short of it is that I used my Roman connections to have the accusations against you rescinded." He fell quiet.

It was that moment in which she turned to face him. She sensed there was more he was unwilling to share but considered it best to be grateful and not to pry. "You promised me a story."

"I did indeed." He glanced up at the sky. "A glorious story."

"What did my brother's disciples say when you told them?"

A shadow formed across his countenance.

"Saul?"

He slowly lowered his head to meet her gaze. "I attempted to meet with them, but they won't see me." He wiped the length of his face. "They're afraid of me. They don't believe that I'm not the same man I was when I left here."

"Even I can see you're not."

"You're a much more trusting soul than the rest of them."

An idea wiggled its way into her mind. "Come. I have a plan." She started walking toward the Muster Gate.

"Where are we going?"

"You'll see." She picked up her pace, her aching legs screaming to run. "Follow me."

Saul hurried after her.

Salome bolted down the enormous marble staircase until she entered the Kidron Valley. "I know someone who can help." Her toes hit the baking sands of the valley path.

"Who?"

"Just wait."

Salome led Saul through the valley and toward the beautiful olive grove nestled on the side of the Mount of Olives. She followed the path leading to the entrance of the garden and hesitated.

Saul kept walking ahead but stopped when she didn't keep going. "What is it?"

"This is where it happened."

Saul looked up at the swaying olive trees. "We're going to the home of the olive oil merchant's widow?"

"Miriam." She took a small step forward, putting her hand on an olive tree. Its rough bark was warm against her palm. "It looks the same as it did three years ago." She rubbed the trunk. "As if time has not affected this place at all."

"You think this woman can help?"

Salome patted the tree. "I do. Come." She continued on the path toward Miriam's home.

The stone house sat neatly kept in the grove's heart. Sounds of merriment filled the air around it, calling Salome nearer. As she approached, it was Saul who hesitated this time. She turned back toward him.

"What if she won't help either?"

"She will." Salome waved him forward.

Saul stepped closer but kept his distance.

Salome came to the open door and called out, "Blessings to the owner of this home."

Sounds of shuffling and footsteps came from inside until a form filled the doorway.

"Salome?" The place between John Mark's eyebrows squeezed together to create a deep crease.

She took in the sight of a man, no longer a grieving young boy. The stubble on his chin had become almost a full beard. He'd grown taller and his shoulders had spread. "John Mark, is that you?"

"Salome! It's Salome. Ima, get out here!" He moved to envelop her in an embrace, lifting her to her toes.

The air rushed out of her lungs at his crushing hold.

"I can't believe it's you." He set her down gently. "I thought we'd never see you again."

A large tear rolled down his cheek, and he brushed it away. "Ima and I have prayed for you every day."

Miriam made it to the door. "Salome." She wrapped her in as tight a hold as John Mark. "Oh, sweet girl. It's so wonderful to see you." She released her only enough to wipe the hair from her face and kissed her cheeks. Placing a hand on one cheek, she squeezed. "How did you ever manage to leave that awful place?"

Salome slid her eyes toward Saul.

Miriam's attention followed, and she gasped. She grabbed Salome and pulled her behind herself. "John."

The obedient son put himself between Saul and the two women. "We have no business with you, Pharisee."

Saul took a step back.

"Shalom." Salome wiggled free of Miriam's grasp and stepped between John Mark and Saul, throwing her hands between them. "Please listen."

John Mark pressed against her hand. "This is the man who put you in chains."

"I know who he is. Look at him," Salome pleaded. "He's not the same."

John Mark glanced over her head.

Salome watched his features shift.

"What's happened to him?"

She turned to Saul. "Give him a chance to tell us." She returned her attention to John Mark. "He's promised it's a good story."

John Mark lowered his gaze. "It better be." He looked at Saul. "Don't make me regret welcoming you into this house."

Saul nodded and approached slowly.

John Mark moved Salome into Miriam's arms and led them inside.

Salome stepped into the stone house and all the memories of her days of sharing her brother's stories came flooding back over her. How many people had come during those days to hear her words? How many people did Miriam feed from her table? How many souls had accepted Jesus as Messiah?

"Here." Miriam fluffed her favorite blue pillow and patted it down. "You sit right here, Salome."

She obeyed and settled on the plump material. It was the first time in three years her backside had felt the softness of a pillow. She melted into the luxury. Every muscle and joint felt more tired than ever before.

Miriam fluttered about the room, bringing offering after offering of food and placing them at Salome's feet. "You look like the wind could blow you away." She put down another bowl. "Eat. Eat."

Salome bowed her thanksgiving and added a prayer before tasting Miriam's delicacies.

John Mark produced a pillow for Saul and took one of his own and placed it between Salome and the Pharisee. "Now," he folded his muscular arms across his chest, "Salome says you've got a story to share."

"It's true." Saul bowed toward Miriam as she placed a single bowl of dried figs beside him. "I don't know if anyone will believe it, but it's true."

"Then speak, and we will be happy to judge you."

"John Mark." Salome nudged him with her elbow. "Be kind."

"I don't blame him." Saul shook his head. "I'd be leery of myself were I in your place." He looked up at the ceiling. "I've caused so much pain, and I hope to be given the chance to set things right."

"Go on, Saul." Salome waved him on.

Saul picked up a fig and twisted it between his fingers. "As I was on my way to Damascus, about midday, a brilliant light from heaven suddenly shone around me. I fell to the ground and heard a voice speaking to me, 'Saul, Saul, why are you persecuting me?' I answered, 'Who are you, Lord?' And He said to Me, 'I am Jesus of Nazareth, whom you are persecuting.'"

Salome put a hand to her chest. "You saw my brother?"

"As clearly as I see you." Saul looked at her. "Though a blinding light surrounded Him. Those who were with me saw the light but did not understand the voice. And I said, 'What shall I do, Lord?' And the

Lord said to me, 'Rise, and go into Damascus, and there you will be told all that is appointed for you to do.'"

"You were hunting Way Followers and Simon."

He hung his head. "I was so angry after what happened to Penelope." He looked up to meet Salome's gaze. "The light of Jesus blinded me. I couldn't see anything. The Temple guards I took with me had to take me by the hand and lead me into Damascus."

"So, you did make it there."

"Blinded, but yes. The guards took me into the home of a man named Judas. I was there for three days and took no food or drink. All I did was beg Adonai to end my life. I'd seen who I truly was in the light of Adonai's holiness, and I didn't measure up."

"What happened after three days?"

"A man named Ananias, a devout man and well-spoken of by all the Jews in Damascus, came to the house seeking me. He had Simon with him."

Salome edged closer. "You saw Simon?"

"He wasn't happy about Ananias coming to me. I think he went along as protection for the old man. But Ananias had been instructed in a vision to visit me. He touched my eyes and said, 'Brother Saul, receive your sight.'" Tears raced down Saul's cheeks. "He called me 'brother.' I couldn't believe it. I was there to arrest him and the others, and the man called me 'brother.'"

Salome reached for Saul. "Go on."

"At the very moment of his prayer, I received my sight and saw Ananias standing before me. He said, 'The God of our fathers appointed you to know His will, to see the Righteous One and to hear a voice from His mouth; for you will be a witness for Him to everyone of what you have seen and heard. And now why do you wait? Rise and be baptized and wash away your sins, calling on His name.'"

"Did you obey?"

"Ananias took me down to the river himself to baptize me."

Joy and thankfulness rose inside Salome. The man who held the title of Slaughterer sat beside her changed. He was no longer a hunter; he was a sibling. She lifted her eyes. "Thank you, Adonai, for our new brother." Her gaze came down slowly. "But wait, you said all that happened when you left Jerusalem. That was three years ago. Where have you been since then?"

CHAPTER 25

Salome waited for Saul to answer.

"After I regained my sight, I began teaching in the synagogues of Damascus. Of course, the people didn't receive me well at first. There were already murmurings about my presence in the city. They knew why I'd come. But eventually, I won them over. They saw how Jesus had changed me."

"So, you've been in Damascus for three years?"

"I would visit back and forth. I spent most of my time in the surrounding region, traveling from city to city, sharing my experience with anyone who would listen."

"And what about Simon?"

"Your brother found a place among the Followers in Damascus." He smiled. "Eventually, finding a place among the household of Ananias as well."

"What does that mean?"

"He wed Ananias' daughter, and they were expecting their first child when I escaped."

Images of Simon leapt to her mind. She couldn't imagine her untamable brother wed and preparing to be an abba. "Wait." Saul's words washed over her again. "Escaped?"

"The Syrian officials were against me. They didn't want their citizens to become Way Followers. There was a plot forming to capture me, so Simon and Ananias lowered me out of the city by night in a basket. Then I made my way back here to Jerusalem."

Salome turned to John Mark. "You have to admit, that's a pretty good story."

John Mark lifted his chin. "I still don't see why you brought him here."

Salome shifted her gaze to Miriam. "I was hoping you could convince Barnabas to bring Saul to James and Peter. If they would listen to anyone, it would be him. If Saul can win over Barnabas, he can win the rest."

Miriam turned to John Mark. "What do you think?"

John Mark set dark eyes on Salome. "If Salome believes Saul's story, that's good enough for me. I'll fetch Barnabas." He rose and headed for the door.

Salome lifted her cup to drink. She emptied it and the rest of the bowls, listening to Saul share more of his adventures while they waited for John Mark to return.

When John Mark arrived with Barnabas, Saul recounted his story again.

Barnabas looked at each of the women. "I think he speaks truth." He returned his attention to Saul. "The man certainly has the fire in his eyes." He turned to Salome. "What is it you need?"

"We need you to take Saul to James and Peter. I know they will listen to you."

"You've not gone to see your family since your release?"

Salome flinched and turned to Saul. "I needed to help my new brother."

"Then we should make haste." Barnabas headed for the door. "I know where to find them."

Barnabas led them through the olive grove, the garden, the valley, and the city of Jerusalem.

Waves of exhaustion crashed over Salome. This was the most she'd walked or used her tired muscles after years crammed into a cell.

Miriam came to support her. "After this, we are going to tend to you."

All Salome could do in response was give an approving hum.

They marched through a gate and toward the Lower City.

Salome dragged weary feet. "We're not going to Priest Theodotos' villa?"

Barnabas moved next to her. "After Saul..." He glanced at Saul. "After the arrests, many of the followers left the city. James and Peter decided it wasn't safe to remain in the villa. They've moved several times in the last few years. But I know where they are. It's not much further."

John Mark came up beside them and whispered, "I still don't know if it's a good idea to be revealing this location, cousin."

"We must trust Adonai. He's clearly redeemed Saul. James and Peter need to see him."

They stopped in front of a short wall surrounding a courtyard.

"I'll go in and let them know what's coming." Barnabas opened the gate. "You stay here." He closed the gate behind himself and went to the door.

Salome looked at Saul. He shifted from one foot to the next as beads of sweat formed at the corners of his forehead.

"Shalom," she whispered. "My brother will hear you."

As if hearing his name, James appeared in the courtyard. "Salome?"

She opened the gate and ran into her brother's arms. "Oh James, I've missed you." He lifted her and twirled her until she felt sick.

"We've been so worried." He pressed his face into her matted hair. "Hiram updated us through his visits, but we've kept the others away for protection." He set her down and held her out. "My dear sister, you're in desperate need of a scrubbing."

She laughed, gazing down at the rags of her filthy tunic and muddy body. "I sure do. But first." She turned toward Saul. "There's someone here you must see."

James lowered his mouth to her ear. "This isn't a good idea, Salome. You don't know what he's done."

"I, above many others, know exactly what he's done." She squinted at her older brother. "I've sat in chains for teaching about Jesus, and Saul is the reason. Please, James, you must hear him."

"It's true." Barnabas moved to stand next to Salome. "I've heard his testimony, and it's not one to be missed. Please, James, hear him."

James looked at each of them before glaring at Saul. "Step forward."

Obeying, Saul entered the courtyard and closed the gate behind himself.

James wrapped his arm around Salome's waist as if she'd flee at any moment. "Speak."

Saul cleared his throat and recounted his travel to Damascus and the light of Jesus that blinded him with the truth.

Salome kept her eyes on James while Saul spoke. As fascinating as Saul's story was, it was her older brother that held her attention. She noticed flecks of gray at his temples and the edges of his beard that weren't there the last time she saw him. His once proud shoulders slumped some. It was as if the weight of his responsibilities was draining his strength and the color from his hair. Hiram had told her about James' position as a leader among the Way Follower gatherings in Jerusalem. Salome worried if the burden was too much for her brother.

"He's seen Jesus." Barnabas' declaration brought her back to the moment. "Jesus has spoken to Saul, and he's preached boldly not only in Damascus but in many of the surrounding regions for the last three years."

Salome waited for James to speak.

James pulled at his beard.

She watched his jaw muscles flick back and forth as if ruminating on Saul's story.

"I believe him," James declared. "We must bring him to the others."

"Welcome, brother Saul." Barnabas extended his arms.

Saul accepted the embrace and followed him into the house, along with John Mark and Miriam.

Salome stepped to follow.

"Wait." James kept his hold on her. "How did you come to be free?"

She lifted a palm. "Saul, of course. He secured my pardon when he came back to Jerusalem."

James' eyes watered. "Why didn't you come to us immediately after your release?"

"I didn't know where you were." She lifted her shoulder. "I also needed to help Saul."

"You?" James' head dropped to the side.

"Saul said you wouldn't see him, so I took him to Barnabas' family. I knew he could convince you to hear Saul."

"I would've heard you."

It was her turn for mist to form in her eyes. "It's been so long; I didn't know if you'd forgotten me."

"Never." He pulled her into a warm embrace.

"We've prayed every day for your return."

She melted into James' strong arms.

"But," he held her out, "you certainly need bathing before you see any of the others."

She chuckled. "And a new tunic if you've got one."

CHAPTER 26

Entering the small dwelling, the scents of burning coal and spices hit Salome, tempting her with promises of warmth and sustenance. Though she was full of Miriam's provisions, the inviting smells sent her stomach rumbling. Nearing the open area, Salome saw a woman stroking the cooking fire. "Elissa?"

Her sister-in-law straightened and turned around. "Salome?" She dropped her stick and cleared the space between them.

Salome held on tight to Elissa. Though each hug aggravated her wounded and weary body, she wouldn't exchange them for anything.

"Praise Adonai for answered prayers." Elissa wiped her damp face. Her countenance shifted, and she swatted at Salome. "How dare you leave me with an inconsolable Hiram. That man has been driven to near madness since your arrest."

Joy and sorrow mingled within Salome at Elissa's playful demeanor. "He's visited me more than the rest of you."

"Who do you think kept us from doing so?" Elissa put a fist on her wide hip. "I had a bag all packed when we received word of your arrest, and Hiram forbade me from even stepping foot near the Temple prison."

"When have you ever obeyed Hiram?"

Elissa dropped her fist. "I shouldn't have." She

reached out to squeeze Salome's arm. "I should have gone running to that cell when I heard what Saul had done."

Salome watched waves of pain and grief rise in Elissa's eyes. "I'm free now. Let's focus on that."

"Ima, ima, ima," a shrill cry came bounding into the room, followed by a young boy. "Look what I got." He stopped in the doorway with his hands tightly closed and extended.

Taking in the small boy, Salome couldn't deny who he was even though she hadn't seen him since he was nursing at his mother's chest. "Joshua?"

The boy, who matched his father in everything but height and beard, tilted his head to the side. "Who are you?"

Elissa came near to him and knelt to meet his eyes. "This is your abba's sister, Salome."

Joshua stared at her for several moments before lifting his hands. "Then I guess it's alright for you to see too."

Salome lowered herself. "I'd be honored."

Opening his hands just enough, Joshua revealed his hidden treasure.

Peering into the space between his plump fingers, Salome saw two large brown eyes staring back at her. The little speckled creature reminded her of Maximus.

"It's a moon lizard." Joshua beamed. "I catched him all by myself."

"I caught him," Elissa corrected.

Joshua glared at his mother. "No, I caught him."

Elissa chuckled and sighed. "Why don't you return

our little friend to wherever you found him?"

"But I wanna keep him." Joshua's lower lip crept past his upper lip.

Elissa returned a fist to her hip. "Not in this house. Now, go on." She shooed him with both of her hands. "Take him back outside before you let him loose."

Joshua turned away but lifted his head over his shoulder. "Are you staying, *Doda*?"

Salome put a hand to her chest, capturing the moment in her heart and mind; the first time she heard her nephew call her aunt. "Of course, I'm staying.

He gave an agreeable nod and left the house.

Elissa picked up her stick and returned to her fire. "That boy is a joy and a challenge."

"Most boys are." Salome smiled as a flood of memories of her older brothers came rushing over her. "But they also bring some of the sweetest moments to your life."

"Speaking of boys." Elissa turned away from the simmering flames. "Have you been to see your other brothers?"

Salome shook her head. "Miriam's was my first stop, and Barnabas brought us here. Where can I find them?"

"Jude is most likely in his synagogue."

"His synagogue?"

"Oh." Elissa put a hand to her cheek, her expression turning somber. "That's right, you've been...away. Rabbi Ethan has gone on to be with Jesus. Jude took over his synagogue."

Joy wrapped around Salome's already expanding

heart. "Truly? Jude's a rabbi of his own synagogue?"

Elissa nodded enthusiastically, her eyes lighting up. "A great one. We attend as much as we are able."

A thought crossed Salome's mind. "And Arava?"

"Faithfully serves beside her husband. She's even taken to teaching her gestures to other people without hearing to help them communicate."

"You jest."

"I don't." Elissa chuckled softly, stirring the flames of her coal fire. "They invite some of them over to their home after meetings so Arava can gesture Jude's message to those who can't hear it."

"What a wonderful blessing."

"It truly has been." Elissa clasped her hands in front of her, then tilted her head, studying Salome. "I know Jude would love to see you." She paused, her gaze sweeping Salome from head to toe. A frown furrowed her brow. "Well, after we get you cleaned up."

Salome glanced down at her rat-bitten tunic, flea-bitten flesh, and the matted ends of her long hair. "I'd be grateful."

Elissa held out her hand. "Come with me."

Miriam moved toward them, closing the private space of the sisters. "I can help."

Willingly, Salome followed Elissa and Miriam to one of the back rooms. Inside, she reached to remove her worn-out tunics. Lifting the materials over her head, she heard Elissa gasp. She flinched and turned to face her sister-in-law.

Tears raced down Elissa's face. "What did they do to you?"

Salome peeked over her shoulder but could not take in the full view of what the other two women must have seen. "I didn't yield to their demands of my silence. These are the scars I share with my brother...brothers."

Miriam stepped forward. She traced one scar with a delicate touch. "You endured all this?"

"And more." Salome tucked her head. "But Saul helped me see these past three years as a kind of substitutionary sacrifice for the crimes Lydia and Simon committed." She looked up into their ashen faces. "They were guilty, but I paid their debt. Like Jesus did for us."

Tracing another scar, Miriam nodded. "'Surely he has borne our griefs and carried our sorrows; yet we esteemed him stricken, smitten by God, and afflicted. But he was pierced for our transgressions; he was crushed for our iniquities; upon him was the chastisement that brought us peace, and with his wounds we are healed.'"

Salome recognized the words of the prophet Isaiah. "'All we like sheep have gone astray; we have turned—every one—to his own way; and the Lord has laid on him the iniquity of us all.'"

Elissa wiped her face. "Come now. We have much to do."

The two women stripped, scrubbed, and scented Salome. Warm water, aromatic oils, and lotions were a balm to her skin and soul. When their treatments were complete, they slipped a freshly laundered tunic over Salome's head.

"Here." Elissa placed a pillow in the center of the room.

Salome lowered herself onto it. Adjusting, she wondered if she would ever get used to the softness of a cushioned seat again.

Elissa and Miriam set to work breaking up the matted mess of Salome's hair. Gently, they pulled apart knots and combed out dirt and debris. The two women chatted as they forged through the tangles.

Salome sat soaking in their words and their fellowship. She closed her eyes, lifting prayers for the women and men she left behind in the cells. If only they would soon know this level of freedom.

She looked around. "Where is my ima?"

"Mary is with John." Elissa tugged at an especially difficult knot. "He still takes his role as her appointed caregiver seriously."

"I see not much has changed since I've been away."

"Much has changed." Miriam bent to enter her line of sight. "We still receive reports of people changed by your words and your faith."

Salome's heart thudded. "Changed?"

"Yes," Elissa answered, her voice full of awe. "It's not only those that have been released from prison, like you. There are others, ones who left Jerusalem after their arrests, who've spread Jesus' teachings they learned from you. Many of them have come to us and told us how your courage inspired them to stand up in faith, even in the face of persecution. And they still speak of you, of the way you gave them hope."

Miriam nodded, her eyes glistening with unshed tears. "I spoke with a man just last week who was in prison with you. He said you never stopped praying, even after your worst beatings. He said he could feel Adonai's presence when you prayed, and it made him believe again. Now, he's traveling with a group of believers, spreading the message you taught him."

Salome's chest tightened as she absorbed their words. "But I've done nothing...I've just...endured. How could I have had such an impact?"

Elissa smiled, her face glowing with affection. "It's not what you've done, Salome. It's who you are. You've been a living example of Jesus' love. Even in the darkness, you shone His light. Your faith, your courage...they're what have inspired us all."

"Even when it feels like nothing will change," Miriam added softly, "you taught us that our faith is the most powerful thing we have. Not our freedom, not our lives, but our unshakable trust in Adonai."

Salome closed her eyes for a moment, feeling the weight of their words sink into her heart. The pain in her body was nothing compared to the warmth that filled her chest, a deep, abiding peace.

CHAPTER 27

When Elissa announced Salome's hair was as good as it was going to get, she rubbed olive oil into her scalp.

The intoxicating aroma of cinnamon tickled Salome's nose. Not only did the bark have healing properties, but its scent brought comfort along with it.

After working the oil into Salome's head, Elissa formed a simple braid and tied the ends with a strip of leather. "Finished." She lifted a small piece of polished bronze to Salome.

Peering into the reflective metal, Salome didn't recognize the woman staring back at her. Her cheeks were hollow. Her skin was pale. Bite marks marred her flesh. But her eyes...there were still the flames of Jesus among them. She turned the metal over and handed it back to Elissa. "Can we go see Jude now?"

"Jude?" Saul's form filled the doorway. "My sister's husband?"

"The same." Elissa rose. "Salome needs to see her family."

Saul hung his head. "As do I."

Salome rose, her legs feeling even more like watery weights. "Join us."

Peeking from under bushy eyebrows, Saul raised his head some. "Do you think she'd see me?"

"Let's find out together."

Salome slipped on a pair of Elissa's sandals and followed Barnabas through the Lower City to the small synagogue once led by Rabbi Ethan.

The square building sat nestled among the busy streets of Jerusalem like a nest among branches. Salome knew this was a place where Jews and Way Followers could hear the words of Moses and the Prophets as well as how Jesus was the answer to their proclamations.

Pushing open the wooden door, Barnabas entered first, followed by Salome and John Mark behind her. Saul trailed at a distance.

Salome stepped into the open room and was immediately welcomed by the embrace of burning olive oil from lamps and the undeniable scent of parchment.

"Shalom," Barnabas called out.

Jude appeared from the back room. "Shalom, how may I assist—" He halted his approach. "Salome?"

"Shalom, brother."

Hurried steps brought Jude across the room and near her. He stopped to stand over her. "I can't believe it." He took her by the arms and bent to kiss both her cheeks. "You're free."

Salome melted into his welcome, returning her own kisses to his cheeks. The smell of parchment and ink wafted off him as if he'd fused with his scrolls.

Jude held onto her arms. "Wait." He released her

to hurry toward the back room. After only a moment, he returned with Arava.

Tears welled in Salome's eyes as she took in the woman. All the memories of the frightened young girl's abandonment by her family and community came rushing back to her. The hours of practice spent developing gestures to reach her in her silence and to give her a voice. Here she stood, shoulders back, chin high, and countenance dripping with joy and confidence. She picked up the hem of her tunic and ran straight into Salome's arms.

The force of her delight nearly knocked Salome to the ground. Her knees buckled at the weight, but she pressed herself into her friend's love.

In a heartbeat, Jude tore Arava from her arms.

"What's he doing here?" Jude yanked Arava behind himself, staring at Saul.

Salome's arms ached with emptiness. "Don't be frightened." Her heart squeezed, watching fear rise in Jude's stance. "Give us a moment to explain."

"How dare you bring him here." Jude shuffled a step back.

Arava's hand came over his shoulder, halting him.

Jude flicked his gaze at her.

With a few pats on his shoulder, Arava moved around him.

He grabbed her arm and violently shook his head at her.

Arava looked past him to Saul, then back to her

husband. She nodded once and patted his hand on her arm before moving slowly toward her brother.

Jude reluctantly released her arm but kept to her back. His glare stayed pinned on Saul.

With light steps, Arava approached Saul. She slowly raised her arm toward his face.

Salome noted red creeping up the side of Saul's neck and his eyes slowly closed. When Arava made it to her brother, she cupped his cheek with her hand. Tears streamed down Saul's face, but he didn't open his eyes. With her thumb, Arava caressed the place under Saul's eyes, wiping away his tears. His lips quaked. His eyes shot open.

A slow smile raised the sides of Arava's mouth. She rocked back on her heels, putting just enough space between them. She lowered her hand to point at Saul's chest, then held out one open hand and used the first finger of her other hand to press each finger down, one at a time.

Saul shook his head and gazed over to Jude. "What's she saying?"

Before Jude could open his mouth, Salome answered, "You. Count."

Arava nodded, repeating the gestures to Saul.

Fresh tears cascaded down Salome's face. "She's saying you matter."

More gestures came faster, and Arava kept pointing to Saul's eyes.

He looked at Salome for interpretation.

She lifted her shoulder. "I guess she's had a lot more practice in the years I've been away."

Jude moved toward them. "She's saying she sees fire in his eyes."

Arava nodded, repeating the gestures once more.

"We saw it too." Salome turned toward Jude. "Please hear his story and share it with Arava. She must know what's happened to her brother."

With a cooling glare, Jude looked at Saul. "He's seen Jesus, hasn't he?"

"You know?"

"No." Jude dropped his gaze to Salome. "But I saw the same look in James' eyes when he saw our resurrected brother. It is undeniable." He waved toward one side of the room. "Come, Saul. We'll sit, and you can tell us all about it."

Saul followed Jude toward the stone steps, but Salome reached for Arava's attention. Bits and pieces of their gestures came back to her mind, but nothing seemed good enough to express all the emotions welling up inside her. She looked down at her sandaled feet, trying to pluck out just the right words.

Lifting her gaze, she noticed Arava's fingers. She flicked a glimpse up into Arava's eyes and lifted a brow before reaching for her hands and holding up Arava's darkened fingers. It took only a brief inspection to realize the cause behind the odd discoloration. Salome had seen it enough times on her brother's fingers.

"Write?" Salome spoke the word as clearly as she

could, knowing Arava had learned to communicate first by watching mouths, and pointed to the girl's dark fingertips.

She nodded several times and twisted her stained fingers around Salome's wrist, dragging her toward the back room.

In the small chamber, a low table held stacks of parchments and ink wells.

Arava shuffled through one stack and produced a scrap of papyrus which she handed to Salome.

In clear marks, Salome read the words aloud, "'My lips will pour forth praise, for You teach me Your statutes. My tongue will sing of Your word, for all Your commandments are right.'" She lowered the parchment and stared into Arava's eyes. "You've learned to sing."

Arava nodded and gestured to the marks and then at her lips.

Salome read them silently again, taking in each stroke of Arava's handwriting. "You taught the mute to sing Your praises, Lord."

"Salome!"

Glaring at the opening of the meeting room, Salome heard the voice that blasted in her ears like a shofar. "Hiram," his name came out as a whisper at first. She returned the parchment to Arava and rushed toward the sound of his voice. "Hiram?" She collided with the broad chest of the man whose kindness and tenderness helped her survive three years in the belly of Sheol. Muscled arms wrapped around her.

"Salome."

She heard her name against her hair like the whisper of a prayer and its answer in the same breath. She squeezed his side, drawing him closer.

"Why didn't you come to me?" He nuzzled her neck. "Elissa came to my booth a-a-and told me you'd been freed," his voice shook, matching the quake in his arms. "She told me you were visiting everyone in the city before me."

Salome chuckled. "Elissa doesn't speak truth. I simply came to see my family."

Hiram eased back just enough to put space between their faces. "That's what I want to be; I want to be your family, Salome."

Words escaped her. "Hiram, I—"

"Today, Salome."

She saw hunger grow in his eyes.

"I've waited over three years to call you my bride. I'm not waiting another moment."

Her stomach tightened. "I don't understand."

"What do you think all those gifts of food and money for protection were for?"

Every one of Hiram's visits came back to her. The fleeting moments of his presence in her darkest places, the nourishment that sustained her at the lowest points, the sound of her name on his lips…these had been used by Adonai to preserve her, but she never saw them for anything more than a friend's kindness.

"What are you saying?"

"The day I saw you…" His bottom lip disappeared as he chewed on his words. "That day I visited, and you were barely surviving, I spoke to my father and told him I was heading back to my grave if I didn't have you in my life." He shook his head. "We gathered a bride price and took it to James."

Salome blinked several times. "My brother accepted a *mohar* on my behalf?"

"Probably took some convincing from Elissa." He smiled. "But he did. Many of the following provisions were part of your *mattan*."

"Your bridegroom gifts? But why?"

He dropped his head to the side. "It's not like I could've brought you jewelry or fine clothes. They would have done you no good in a cell. I provided what you needed, so that one day…" He drew her closer. "…one day we could be wed."

Tears stung her eyes. "I never thought that day would come."

"I did." His cheeks warmed with color. "When you enter the room, my sorrow dies, then when you leave, it awakens again and again." He shook his head. "Every time I left you in that prison, a piece of me died. But I knew one day Adonai would restore you, and we would be together. That is," he dropped his gaze, "if you'll have me."

"Hiram." She wrapped her arms around his neck. "If you'll have me, I'll have you."

CHAPTER 28

After much convincing, Salome got Hiram to allow a few days to prepare for a wedding feast.

With her family scattered through Jerusalem, Salome elected to stay with Miriam before joining Hiram's household. She sat quietly at the low table, listening to Miriam fuss about the room, adding her own preparations for the upcoming feast. Salome's fine tunic and elaborate decorations prevented her from joining Miriam. If she got near food, she would ruin all the women's hard work in preparing her for tonight.

There was a lamp in front of her on the table. The smell of perfectly cultivated olive oil rose with the small flame that provided light.

Salome watched the flicker dance for several moments. It was wonderful and oddly strange to be back under her friend's roof. She'd been taken captive in this place; however, before that, this was where she felt most herself.

Despite Saul's attempts to snuff out the flame of Way Followers, when he left for Damascus and didn't return, Miriam welcomed people into her home once more. The thriving collection grew by feeding off the stories they could remember Salome telling and the ones they gathered from listening to Peter and the other disciples.

Her thoughts drifted to her dispersed family. She missed them terribly while she was imprisoned and loved Elissa's reports on each of Salome's siblings.

James was busy keeping a shepherd's eye on the numerous flocks of Way Followers in Jerusalem, along with running his own home with Elissa and young Joshua. Joseph had taken Naavah to Nazareth, far away from her brother's wicked influence. Assia had welcomed them back to the village with arms filled with Hadassah and a son they named Joseph. Jude was hard at work filling his rabbi's sandals with Arava at his side. Lydia had settled in Antioch with Nicolaus and baby Stephen. And, according to Saul, Simon was thriving in Damascus and his wife Rachel was expecting their first child. Their mother, Mary, was still under the watchful care of John, and they spent much of their days traveling to neighboring areas to speak about Jesus. Her oldest brother was exactly where He deserved to be, seated at the right hand of Adonai.

As much as the thoughts of her family brought joy and comfort, her heart ached for those she left behind the prison bars. Those who would not know the warmth of an oil lamp or family presence this day.

Her attention returned to the flickering lamp before her. Its wild movements reminded her of the tongues of fire that danced above her head on the day of Pentecost. The warmth of the tongue as it filled her from the inside out brought with it a peace she'd never felt before that moment.

She closed her eyes and allowed the memory to wash over her again. When she opened her eyes, the flame was slowly growing dim, showing the oil was running low. She reached over and snuffed out the flame with her fingers, thankful the one inside her would never succumb to the same fate.

Refilling the oil, she trimmed the wick and lit the flame from the cooking fire. Jesus' story of the ten virgins fluttered across her mind. She wanted to be like the wise women who had enough oil while they waited for the bridegroom to arrive.

Just don't wait too long, brother.

An image of a decorated bridegroom floated to the top of her thoughts. She imagined what Hiram would look like when he appeared tonight to claim her. Though the arrival of the bridegroom was intended to be kept secret, Salome knew Hiram would wait no longer. No amount of feast preparations could keep him away. There was nothing left for Salome to do besides wait.

The light from the window faded, but the sounds of bustling outside rose.

"He's coming," Elissa called from outside.

Salome's heart picked up its pace. She wiped her damp palms on her tunic. What was there to be nervous about? Hiram was a good man who would care deeply for her. She cared deeply for him and couldn't wait to be his completely. Still, the anticipation of his arrival sent flutters to her stomach. Thankfully, the feeling wasn't the same as the sting of hornets when she spoke to gatherings.

The door opened all too quickly, and Hiram filled the room with his presence.

Salome rose to greet him, barely able to see Hiram through the sheer veil that covered her face. She itched to tear the material from her head and drink in the full sight of her bridegroom, but she had to be patient.

He came closer and slowly lifted the veil, giving her a broad smile as a greeting.

Salome returned his greeting with a wide grin of her own.

"That's enough," Miriam ordered.

Hiram dropped the veil back into place.

"You two will have plenty of time to stare at each other after the feast." Miriam neared Salome and put a gentle hand under her elbow. "Everyone's waiting for us."

Hiram made his way back to the door.

Salome followed with the support of Miriam on one side and Elissa on the other. Arava assumed the place behind them, forming a female guard around Salome as they marched behind Hiram.

While the processional made their way through the grove, Salome absorbed the beauty of the garden. Green leaves shimmered in the moonbeams, insects added their songs to the merriment, and the fragrance of flowers mingled with the scented wedding guests.

They continued across the valley, made it to the city gates, and proceeded through the Lower City until they reached Theodotos' villa in the Upper City.

Entering the large dwelling felt like coming home. Salome took in the sounds of instruments and people urging her toward the next steps of her life.

Rabbi Jude led the couple in their marriage blessings, and the entire gathering of family and Way Followers joined the feasting and celebrating.

People passed Salome from embrace to embrace while whispering blessings in her ear and leaving joyful kisses on her cheeks. They shared food, told stories, and created new memories in the hours that followed.

The first moment Salome had to herself, she stared around the open courtyard at all the people who held a special place in her heart. Though many were missing, she knew each one was exactly where Adonai needed them. But one face leapt to the front of her thoughts.

Rhoda. The chains of Sheol still bound the young woman. Saul could not secure her release with her family's debt still hanging around her neck.

Miriam moved toward her. "What are you doing here?" She lifted her cup toward the gathering. "You should be soaking in all the joy."

"I am." She couldn't keep the sorrow from her voice.

With a tilt of her head, Miriam hummed. "What's won your attention away from your wedding feast?"

"Do you remember Rhoda?"

"The thorny girl who attended my synagogue?" Miriam hummed again. "Haven't seen her in some time."

"That's because she was arrested that day in your house."

"Oh." Miriam moved her cup to her chest. "I was unaware."

"She's still there."

"In that awful prison? How dreadful." Miriam reached out to grip Salome's arm. "No wonder your thoughts have drifted."

"She became a tether for me in that place."

"But I thought Saul got most of you out."

"He did." One side of Salome's mouth dropped. "But Rhoda's situation is a little more complicated."

"How so?"

"During her imprisonment, her father died."

"The poor dear."

"And he left behind a great debt. She received word that her mother went back to where her family was from and left Rhoda behind with her father's debt to answer for."

"She just left her daughter in a cell?"

"With little explanation, I suppose it was her only means of survival. But Rhoda was heartbroken. And the debt must be paid before she is freed."

Miriam hummed to herself, working her lips. "Let's pray for Adonai's guidance. I'm sure He will lead us to a path to redeem one of His daughters."

Salome lifted a silent plea for Miriam's words to ring true in her brother's ears. "She will be pleased to hear we are praying for her."

"She will?"

"I'm going back."

A cloud of fear and horror moved across Miriam's face.

"Not as a prisoner, but to provide aid to those imprisoned. I'm going to speak to James about it."

"I don't think that's wise."

"James won't either." Salome chuckled. "But I wouldn't have survived had it not been for Hiram's gifts and visits." She smiled, thinking of each one. "Jesus also told us to do it, and I'm even more convicted to obey Him after being on the other side of those bars."

CHAPTER 29

After a week of feasting and family, Salome settled into her new role as wife. Hiram's parents welcomed her with open arms into their home and life and praised her for giving their son new desires for the future. Her bridegroom had prepared space for her in the modest dwelling and promised her freedom to change anything she desired. She assured him multiple times that what he provided was more than adequate, and she looked forward to building their life together.

She hurried through her morning tasks, so she could visit Hiram's booth on the lower level of the stone building before starting preparations for the latter half of the day.

Descending steps were difficult for her. She stopped halfway down to lean against the wall. Her chest tightened; her head swam. It took some convincing to remind herself she was not descending back into the place where she spent three years locked in irons. She took the last steps slowly, using each one to recite Adonai's promises.

Once her foot hit the bottom, she let out a sigh of relief. Pressing on, she found Hiram sitting on a stool with a large piece of fabric in his lap. His needle was flying through the material.

She stopped to stare before interrupting him. How could she be so favored to call him her own? He deserved a queen, not a former prisoner.

In the same moment of her thought, Hiram raised his attention. Lifting his arm, he beckoned her. "Couldn't spend one day away from me I see."

She giggled and raced into his arms. "I surely couldn't."

He set his work aside and drew her into his lap. "So, my beautiful bride, to what do I owe this visit other than my irresistible company?"

She balanced herself on his leg, drinking in the scents of sweat, leather, and linen. "I wanted to see your booth from this side and visit with you."

"You are more than welcome, my love, to visit me anytime you wish."

She peered at the piece of fabric. "What are you working on?"

"A sail." He stretched for it, being careful to keep her perfectly balanced. "Would you like to see how it's done?"

"Could I?"

"You're a tentmaker's wife now. No time like the present to learn what your husband does." He settled the sail on her lap and described his stitch and the material with which he was working.

A sudden commotion in the street drew both their attention.

Salome leapt off Hiram's lap and leaned over his

working table to get a better view. "What's going on?"

"I'm not sure." Hiram stood beside her. "But I think I see Saul heading this way."

"Saul?" Salome leaned further out. "It sounds like he's being chased by a lion."

"No lion, but there's a crowd following him." He came around the table. "Wait here." He rushed down the street toward the source of the unrest.

Salome lifted her hand against the glaring sun, watching for his return.

Hiram hurried back, pushing Saul into the booth. "Get in here and stop all that shouting."

Salome pulled the stool over for him, but Saul paced in a circle around the workspace.

"I can't stop." Saul tore at his hair. "I won't stop."

Hiram attempted to stand in front of him. "At least tell us what happened."

Saul halted. "While I was praying in the temple, I fell into a trance."

"A trance?" Salome pulled the stool over to Saul again, patting the top.

He lowered himself to the edge. "Yes, and in the vision, I saw Jesus."

Salome gasped. "You saw my brother again?"

"This time there was no blinding light." Saul leaned to the side. "But He said, 'Make haste and get out of Jerusalem quickly because they will not accept your testimony about Me.' And I said, 'Lord, they know that in one synagogue after another, I imprisoned and beat those who believed in You. And when the blood of Stephen Your witness was being shed, I was standing by and approving and watching over the garments of those who killed him.'"

The memories of Stephen's horrific death surfaced in Salome's mind. He'd been teaching about Jesus in the synagogue when they dragged him before the council and sentenced him to be stoned. Saul was a newly appointed Pharisee, but he approved of the violence, encouraged it, instead of stopping it. Stephen had recently been betrothed to her sister Lydia and she, in turn, purchased Saul's death from the Zealots. Blood for blood. Only their leader, Barabas, switched the target to Saul's betrothed, a senator's daughter. The death blow came at the hands of her brother Simon, leading to his exile in Damascus. It was a messy ordeal, and one Salome had to remind herself had been redeemed with her days locked away, even if only before Adonai's Judgment Seat.

Saul turned to Salome. "Then Jesus said to me, 'Go, for I will send you far away to the Gentiles.'"

Hiram folded his arms across his chest. "The Gentiles? If your own people will not listen to you, what makes you think Gentiles will?"

Saul rose. "Because the Lord has declared it so."

Salome looked between the two men. "Then what was the uproar Hiram rescued you from?"

"After the vision, I started teaching in the Temple." Saul hung his head. "There were many

Hellenists there, and I was calling them to come out from worshipping Greek idols."

"You picked a fight with the Hellenists in the middle of the Temple?" Hiram wiped the length of his face. "No wonder they were chasing you out of there."

"Please." Saul drew near to him. "You've got to help get me out of Jerusalem. They want to kill me. I know it."

"I guess that's one way to make sure you obey the call to go."

"Hiram!" Salome scolded her husband.

He lifted his shoulder. "It's true."

Salome set a hand on Saul's shaking arm. "James will help." She looked at her husband. "I know he will."

"Then it looks like Saul needs an escort." Hiram waved them out of the booth and set to work unfurling the long canvas to show he was not present to conduct business.

The walk to James' home was uneasy. Hiram led the way, directing Salome and Saul through side streets, hoping to avoid as many people as possible. They neither wanted attention from any Hellenists, nor anyone following them to James' location.

Once there, Salome greeted her brother and pleaded Saul's case.

James listened intently. "Well, brother Saul, I guess this means we need to get you out of Jerusalem. But it certainly sounds like that's Adonai's plan."

Salome turned to Saul. "Where can you go?"

Saul pulled at his beard. "Tarsus. There are many people in my hometown that need to hear the message of Jesus, and since I grew up there, I have many connections."

James shifted his weight, crossing his arms thoughtfully. "Peter and I have some connections in Caesarea. We should be able to escort you that far and see you off to Tarsus."

"Any help would bless me." Saul turned, meeting Salome's gaze with a small, grateful nod. "Thank you for all your help. It seems this is the place we will part."

"I'm very glad you met my brother." Salome touched her hand to her chest, her voice softening, "He makes all the difference."

"He does." Saul's lips curved into a faint smile, though his eyes remained serious.

"I will be praying for your boldness as you tell people about Jesus."

"And I you, Salome."

James gestured toward the door with a curt motion. "If you're ready, I will take you to Peter, and we can take our leave."

Saul sighed. "Another brother helping me escape. I hope this doesn't become a habit." He turned back to Salome. "Shalom," his eyes flamed, "sister."

"Shalom, brother." Salome watched James clap Saul on the shoulder as they turned away.

Stay with him, Jesus. I know You have great plans for Saul; wherever You guide his steps.

Elissa entered the room, wiping her hands on a cloth. "Can I get you something?"

Salome shook her head and turned to her husband. "I'm going to visit Miriam."

Hiram lifted a brow. "The last time I let you do that, I nearly lost you."

"I know." Salome rested her hand on his arm, giving it a reassuring squeeze. "But there has been something weighing heavy on my heart, and I need to speak with her."

Hiram sighed, shaking his head. "There never is any sense in arguing with you. Please, just be careful."

She turned to watch Saul leave with James. "At least I don't have to worry about Saul. My big brother has him all sorted out."

"If you're going to Miriam's, then take this." Elissa grabbed a bag and filled it with items from her table. "Along with my prayers."

"I'm sure she'll welcome this." Salome accepted the bag and left.

Leaving the city and crossing the valley toward the Mount of Olives renewed Salome. The fresh air and bright sky were blessings she counted every moment since she walked out of her cell.

Entering the garden, she felt no pull to visit her brother's tomb. She knew well that it was still empty.

Approaching Miriam's house, she called out a greeting and entered the arms of the olive oil seller.

Miriam kissed both of Salome's cheeks. "What a

delightful surprise."

"I've been doing a lot of praying for Rhoda, and I wanted to see if Adonai had given you any wisdom."

Miriam set her fingertips to her lips, suppressing a grin. She cleared her throat. "Well, actually, I've been praying about her as well, and Adonai showed me what to do."

"Truly?" Salome leaned forward; her brow furrowed. "What is it?"

Miriam turned toward the hallway, beckoning with a hand. "Do you want to tell her, or should I?"

From the darkness, Rhoda stepped forward, folding her arms. "I'm surprised her brother didn't tell her; Jesus talks to her an awful lot."

Salome took in the sight of the woman who shared in the similar sorrow and torment while helping her endure it all. She was not the same physically as the girl she met in the synagogue; time behind bars had withered her once luscious beauty and frame. But here she stood, bathed and dressed in a simple tunic, her face bright, with a hint of mischief.

"Rhoda!" Salome threw her arms around her, pulling her close. "What are you doing here?"

The woman wiggled deeper into her embrace. "Ask Miriam."

Salome looked at Miriam. "What happened?"

"Well, I was praying and praying." Miriam clasped her hands together, her face glowing with excitement. "Then I remembered your story about how your time in chains paid for your brother's and sister's debt."

Salome tilted her head, searching Miriam's face. "And?"

"And I figured if debt was the only thing keeping Rhoda in chains, someone else could pay it. So, I went to the Temple and paid her debt."

Salome's eyes widened as she turned back to Rhoda. "You're free."

"Well…" Rhoda rubbed her arm, glancing at Miriam. "Not exactly."

"In order to get her debt forgiven, we had to agree to a contract. Rhoda will work off her debt to me as a bondservant. When Rhoda has paid her debt, she will be free to choose her next steps."

"Which won't be until I'm ancient." Rhoda's lips twisted into a wry smile. "My family left behind quite the burden."

"But I'm sure it will seem like mere days under Miriam's roof." Salome nudged Rhoda's shoulder playfully.

Rhoda rolled her eyes. "I'm not Jacob waiting for Rachel." She planted her fists on her hips. "I'll be working to win my own hand."

Salome chuckled. "I'm so happy for you both. I know Miriam will be glad of the help, and this lady will bless you." She reached out for Miriam's hand. "I have one request."

"Name it, and it's yours."

"Your olive trees. May I climb them?"

"You want to climb?"

"I'm very good. It's been so long. It would mean the world to me."

"Normally, the young ones only climb them during harvest time." Miriam tapped her chin, considering. "But you have my blessing."

Salome squeezed her arm. "Then I will take my leave, but I promise to return."

"With more stories?" Miriam's eyes sparkled.

"With more stories."

"And one more thing."

"Yes?"

"Call me Mary. It's more fitting now than Miriam."

Salome smiled warmly, embracing her friend again, before rushing out the door.

She hastened through the garden; her gaze examining the trees. A large olive tree stood proud among its brothers, practically calling for her.

At its base, she untied her sandals and reached between her legs to pull through the back end of her long tunic and tucked it firmly into the leather belt around her waist. With loins girded, she took a deep breath and started her ascent.

The rough bark tore at her flesh, but her body held several callouses from her time in chains. She slipped a few times but caught herself, just as Jesus had taught her. With each branch passed, she felt Him urging her on.

Grasping the last branch, she pulled herself to the top of the tree and straddled the limb. She faced Jerusalem and glimpsed the bright, white Temple, which sat like a crown upon the city. While it was a beautiful sight that many Jews traveled to behold, her gaze continued on to the paths leading in multiple directions away from the city. Along them would be multitudes of people who had not yet heard the good news of Jesus.

Breathing in the fresh air and sitting among the green leaves that swayed in the wind, she heard her brother's voice whisper in her soul.

You will be my witness, Lioness.

EPILOGUE

Elissa selected a pomegranate from the stack, pushing its smooth exterior to evaluate its ripeness. Adding it to the others she'd chosen from the fruit seller, she exchanged a fair wage and secured the fruit in her bag.

"I think it's time we head home." She turned but discovered her son was missing. "Joshua?" She spun around, thinking the young boy was simply hiding among the booths.

"Joshua?" Her voice bordered on panic. "Joshua, you come out this instant." She bent to look under a nearby stand.

The fruit seller cleared his throat.

Elissa straightened.

He pointed behind her.

She turned to see her five-year-old son speaking with an older man about a stone's throw away. She marched toward them. "Joshua ben James, what have I taught you about wandering away in the market?" The question came out much harsher than she intended, as evidenced by her son's downcast eyes. She softened and beckoned him with her wiggling finger.

The little boy hurried to her side. "Forgive me, Ima, I was telling someone about my uncle."

Elissa sighed. "Forgive my harshness. I didn't

realize. But come now, we need to get home."

Joshua assumed a comfortable pace beside her. "Tell me another story about Him."

Elissa chuckled as she shifted the satchel on her hip. "Your uncle did many wonderful things. He healed the lame, returned strength to the withered, gave the blind their sight, and even—"

"And even raised the dead!"

Elissa halted in front of her husband, James, who was reaching their gate at the same time as they were.

"Abba!" Joshua rushed toward his father.

James scooped Joshua up into his arms and onto his shoulder in one fluid movement.

Joshua giggled as he settled.

James kissed Elissa. "Shalom, my dear. How was the market?"

"Crowded." She adjusted the heavy bag across her body. "It always is this time of year."

"But where is He?" Joshua asked from his perch. "You said He died, but He didn't stay dead. So how come I've never met Him? How come He doesn't visit us here in Jerusalem?"

Elissa gave James a knowing glance.

James pointed to the sky. "Beyond our vision, in the third heavens, there your uncle sits; waiting."

Joshua gazed up for a few moments with a gaped mouth. "What's He waiting for?"

"He's waiting for all to hear of Him," Elissa explained. "That's the mission He gave us before He left."

James waved his free hand to the sky. "Like scattered stars, your uncles, aunts, and cousins are sharing about your uncle until we've told everyone."

Joshua dropped his head with a pout. "I miss them."

"The Feast is soon." James lifted Joshua's chin. "Perhaps they will return this year for a visit."

"I will ask Adonai to bring them back." Joshua stared at the cloudless sky which was just beginning to shift to an orange hue.

For a few quiet moments, the three of them watched the beautiful display.

Joshua broke the silence, "One day, will I be able to tell others about my uncle in faraway places?"

Elissa reached up to squeeze Joshua's knee. "You already spend all of your time telling others." She let her gaze drop to her husband. "He was talking to a stranger in the market again today."

"I was telling him about my uncle," Joshua defended with a small hand on his hip.

James lifted an eyebrow at Elissa. "We can't hold back the tidal wave that is our son."

Elissa smiled up at her young boy. "I don't think I want to."

James twisted to look at Joshua. "I believe you will get to share with people in faraway places, my son. In fact, you will probably have to do so."

Joshua's little head fell to one side. "Have to?"

"By the time you've grown, everyone in this city will have heard you speak of your uncle." James let out a hardy chuckle.

Elissa shook her head. It was true. Joshua had been sharing stories of his uncle since he could talk. If Adonai kept him in Jerusalem, the entire city would hear his voice, whether or not they wanted to.

James pushed open the gate and waved Elissa inside. He followed her, lifting Joshua from his shoulders and setting him down in the courtyard.

"I want everyone to hear of Him." Joshua put his little hand over his chest. "I feel this push inside to speak about Him."

"That's your gift from Adonai." James knelt to meet his son's eyes. He pointed to his own chest, then to Joshua's. "Adonai flames a fire in there that helps us speak."

Joshua gazed down. "I have Adonai's fire in here?"

Elissa smiled as she knelt beside them. "Yes, you do. So, speak, my son. Tell the world about Jesus."

What To Read Next?

In the raging sea of fear, Epaphroditus finds his faith.

In the bustling colony of Philippi, Epaphroditus, the son of a traveling merchant, finds himself ensnared in the threads of destiny. Blessed with wealth and privilege, his life is shadowed by a prophecy whispered by one of Aphrodite's priestesses: a grim fate aboard a ship awaits Epaphroditus.

Living vicariously through his best friend Luke, a compassionate physician traversing the seas to aid the afflicted, Epaphroditus grapples with the threat of mortality and the uncertainty of his future. When a bold traveler named Paul arrives, bearing tales of a humble carpenter from Nazareth named Jesus, Epaphroditus finds himself drawn into a journey of faith.

Join Epaphroditus on his extraordinary odyssey, where he discovers the transformative power of grace and the strength to battle fear with faith. Dare to embark on a journey that will stir your soul and ignite your faith as the letter of Philippians comes to life in **Leading Philippi**, Book 1 of the *Paul's Patrons series*.

More from Jenifer Jennings:

Special Collections and Boxed Sets
Biblical Historical stories from the Old Testament to the New, these special boxed editions offer a great way to catch up or to fall in love with Jenifer Jennings' books for the first time.

The Rebekah Series: Books 1-3
Faith Finder Series: Books 1-3
Faith Finders Series: Books 4-6
Servant Siblings Series: Books 1-3
Servant Siblings Series: Books 4-7
Paul's Patrons Series: Books 1-3
Paul's Patrons Series: Books 4-6

* * *

The Rebekah Series:
Follow Rebekah on her faith journey from the fields of her homeland to being part of Abraham's family.

The Stranger
The Journey
The Hope

* * *

Find these titles at your favorite retailer or at:
jeniferjennings.com/books

* * *

If this story inspired you, consider sharing your honest thoughts in a review. Your words help spread these stories of faith even further.

About the Author

Jenifer Jennings is a passionate storyteller who brings ancient worlds to life through Biblical historical novels. A devoted student of Scripture since coming to faith in Jesus at seventeen, she holds a bachelor's degree in Women's Ministry and a master's in Biblical Languages. Jenifer is an active member of Word Weavers International, serving as an online chapter president, and a member of American Christian Fiction Writers (ACFW). When Jenifer's not writing, she's on a date with her husband or mothering their two children, a wise-cracking mathematician and a feisty artist.

If you'd like to keep up with new releases, receive spiritual encouragement, and get your hands on a FREE book, then join Jenifer's Newsletter at:
jeniferjennings.com/gift